PRAISE FOR WINTERGLASS

A fairy tale, beautiful like an ice crystal, and razor sharp.

Winterglass is rich with diamondine prose, a scintillant retelling of the Ice Queen that challenges Occidental aesthetics, colonial mentality, and personal identity.

An exquisite gem of a novella. Politics, relationships, and combat presented as a matryoshka, the beauty of which is there's no easy way of telling which shells are within which. Sriduangkaew's sensuous metaphors and elegant imagery are never less than a pleasure to read. Thoroughly recommended.

D1040744

WINTERGLASS

BENJANUN SRIDUANGKAEW

ISBN 978-1937009-62-5 (TPB)

Also available as a DRM-free eBook.

Apex Publications, PO Box 24323, Lexington, KY 40524

Visit us at www.apexbookcompany.com.

ONE TO WAKE

On the night of Nuawa's execution, she saw the Winter Queen for the first time.

The wind was inert and the night ignited by frostworks, teeth of ice biting flowers into the sky. The soldiers had given her something and it made her world both heavy and light, her thoughts dragging behind her like a train. She was thinking not of the ghost-kiln before her—though even at six, she knew what it was and what it did—or even of her mother holding her hand. Instead she was wondering how it was that the queen could walk so evenly and stride so fast in her armor. Frost and iron, the coronet more helm than crown, the sword at her hip as broad as Nuawa. It seemed impossible for a single person to move under so much weight, shoulder so much heft. She imagined then that the queen was iron and rime underneath too, dense strong bones inside the annihilating white of her skin.

A soldier lowered Nuawa into the ghost-kiln's petal mouth. It clenched shut with a small hiss. Later she would try to recall whether the soldier flinched as they did this, whether it mattered to them that she was a child—small for her age—but she would not remember.

Inside the stomach-chamber the air was thick with the smell of dying, the odor of bodies that had already succumbed. Her giving-mother held Nuawa, pressing something sharp into her mouth, whispering that she would live. Nuawa made an obedient noise and swallowed, like a good daughter. It cut going down and filled her mouth with blood, sweet and staccato, though it didn't hurt. Most of her seemed asleep, swaddled in a warm and distant place while here her bare feet turned numb. She lay against her mother's breast and dreamed of a painted blue sky.

After a time, her mother's arms fell limp. The world turned inside Nuawa and the dark scraped at her ankles, her wrists, the base of her skull. It seeped into her mouth and her nose until she felt feverish with secrets. She was a fish, swimming through dark waters. She was a bird, fluttering up a sky she'd only seen as oil on canvas.

When the machine's belly opened, it was still night, or perhaps night again. Nuawa's sense of time had slipped like water on stone. Weak as she was, she looked to make sure, but the queen was no longer about.

People were drawing blanched, drained bodies out of the machine. They pulled. They pried. They wept and carried away their dead. Nuawa waited for her turn without sound or protest. She did not cry for help. Her giving-mother had told her to be quiet until her bearing-mother came.

And she did come, her bearing-mother Indrahi. They were the last. A few other bodies remained, kinless on the gray, frozen ground.

"Are we not taking her home?" Nuawa asked through cracked lips as her bearing-mother lifted her from her giving-mother's breast.

"That is not her. She is gone. From now on you are to understand that she was never your kin." In the cold, her bearing-mother's expression was stone, was ice. She tipped hot ember wine into Nuawa's mouth. "Are you afraid?"

Nuawa considered her fears: freezing to death, falling into the canals where the ice thinned and cracked under her weight, being a disappointment in her arithmetic. But already she was forgetting everything from before her passage through the ghost-kiln, as though it'd purged her, as though it'd remade her anew. Something was gone. Something else was gained. At last she said, "No, I don't think so, Mother." It was strange, to have only one now. One parent, one mother.

Mother took Nuawa's hand. "Good. For your mind is a weapon, Nuawa, and we shall nurture it in the absence of fear. One day you will fire all that you are, like a bullet, into the heart of the Winter Queen."

ONE

THE SEASON'S LAST MATCH BRINGS WITH IT A PRESS OF audience, the mass and noise of them audible even in the preparation vestibule where silence is meant to be the final word. There's nothing for it, Nuawa supposes, as she tightens the seals on her armor and checks her gun one last time. Everything is oiled, ready.

The gladiator's bell rings. The arena gate lifts slowly, a hum of blindfolds and lion helms, a susurrus of tiger tails and specters. She knows the mechanisms are lubricated well, the ghosts fed a rich diet of incense and candlewicks, but the tournament masters like their theatrics.

She steps into a dome of obsidian glass and agate tiles. It is opaque from inside, transparent from the outside. If she falls, they will hear every last noise: the rattle of her final breath and the wet slap of viscera meeting glass, while she will never see their faces. Their rapt faces, empty-eyed, mesmerized by spectacle. So it goes.

The opposite gate unfurls, dove wings and mandarin petals. For half a moment, she sees nothing at all, then discerns the solid outlines of the muzzles, the light-drinking coat, the sleek knotted limbs. They have sent her leopards to fight.

She hears the whirr of their articulated legs, the scrape of their curse-alloyed claws, and knows they are more than animal. Guided by a human mind, potent with thaumaturgy. She counts: four pairs of jade-dark eyes, four tails like whips.

An instant's calculation for angle and trajectory, and she fires. The leopards are fast, upon her far quicker than any human or natural beast could be. Her bullet ricochet off the dome, piercing a leopard's shadow; its flesh corresponds in a rip of meat, a spray of gore. Her second shot catches another in the haunch, interrupting it mid-pounce.

Her drop to the floor is a fraction too late. Claws screech across the metal of her armor, not penetrating but leaving a slick of concentrated grudges: pain flashes down her vertebrae, bright turquoise synesthetic across her vision. Her gauntleted arm is all that keeps her face from being shredded to cartilage and gore.

She pulls a polynomial from her belt, tearing off its safety with her teeth. An implosive flash, more light than heat, blinds the puppeteer behind those feline eyes. Nuawa uses the pause to gain distance, rolling away, drawing her blade. Her sword's beaked shadows click and clatter, a spread of five today: thanks to the lighting, all far longer than the blade itself or her reach. More than sufficient.

Blade shadows roar as they meet the leopards'. Fur tears; arteries rupture and tendons snap.

Nuawa beheads the animals, for theater and for good measure. Even then she half-expects each to get up for a rematch, but apparently they haven't been witched to work beyond stopped hearts and spilled brains. A ground fog of expended power rises, is quick to dissipate. She wonders what shape the puppeteer is in. Incapacitated, with luck. In agony, she hopes.

Her gate lifts. There is no announcement of her victory, no applause. The Marrow is too refined for that.

Back in the vestibule there are attendants waiting, sent by her manager Tezem. One is moon-dusted, the other with a face painted half white and half green. Both are slim, male, adolescent: the diametric opposite of Nuawa's preferences, Tezem's idea of a joke. When they offer her purifying balm and cleansing ointments, she takes the bottles and jars from them. "I'll go up for a bath." Many of Tezem's duelists enjoy being pampered, with attendants to scrub their backs and lather their hair, oil their limbs and perfume their throats. Nuawa prefers to be left well enough alone.

She steps into an elevator; here no sense of drama interferes with function and so the ghosts are efficient, the ride smooth and fast. From overhead, a portrait of the queen looks down, the royal coiffure as iridescent as borealis light. Winter's visage is everywhere, austere in its gauntness, alien in its sclera the black of frostbitten flesh. Speculations as to the queen's origins run abundant, in euphemism and guarded whispers, and most say she is from the distant isle of Yatpun: a snow-woman from permafrost peaks, sick of the mountain gods' tyranny and determined to be lord and deity of her fate. But Yatpun has been inaccessible for centuries behind its event-horizon wall, and if she is indeed from the island nation, the queen is the sole individual alive certain of that truth.

Nuawa presents her credentials, a chalcedony cube at her wrist, to the toothed locks that guard the Marrow's highest, most exclusive floor.

A low humming and a haze of steam. Yifen is coming out of the bath, toweling her hair dry and unselfconsciously nude. At the sight of Nuawa her eyes brighten, her mouth widening into a grin, openly voracious. "Nuawa! I'm just done cleaning up but I don't think I have gotten *all* the grime out of my hair. May I join you?"

Nuawa holds up the purification jars. "Only if you want to risk getting curses on you. This was a dirty fight."

"Please, stuff that weak can't begin to touch me." The other duelist widens her eyes, tilting her head, coquettish. "Or have I begun to bore you?"

In truth, a little. She enjoys Yifen's company well enough most times, but while Yifen is a fine lover, her appetites tend to exceed Nuawa's. Still, a good source of information. "If I tire of you, I would be tiring of life." She disrobes and follows Yifen into the bath. There's only one other occupant, a sour-faced, taciturn duelist from abroad; they don't greet or so much as look up, attention fixed on the pane displaying an intake audition. Nuawa takes a look. Duelists at the Marrow go into each match blind, but the auditions give her some idea of new challenges.

Yifen has opened the jars, spooned out ointment, and warmed it between her tattoo-protected palms. She is inked everywhere, inscribed for stamina and luck, for senses beyond the five physical ones; their first time together was an educational experience for Nuawa. "Scouting for a fling?" Yifen asks, following Nuawa's gaze.

"I'd never slight you to your face." On the pane, Nuawa spots two duelists she's fought in other venues. But most of the aspirants are foreign, a few occidentals whose faces and coloring are only slightly less alien than the queen's. "Why so many travelers?"

"You haven't heard? You must mingle more, visit the commoners once in a moon." Yifen lowers her voice as she spreads purifying balm down Nuawa's spine and hips. "We're getting our first *tribute game*. The winner gets an officer's commission and the queen's general will train them as her very own protégé. Imagine if one of us gets chosen? The first officer ever from Sirapirat."

Despite herself, Nuawa is intrigued. Sirapirat citizens have never been allowed to enlist in the queen's army, let alone rise to an officer. They have to give the queen tribute the same as any other territory, but never in a game, never with the promise of reward. "How is it going to work?"

"Ah, now you're more interested in *that* than in me. How I self-sabotage." Yifen makes a moue. "Our rankings will give us no head start, I fear. All participants will begin equal. The first part will be a survival course. Ten to thirteen winners out of nearly three hundred applicants will then proceed to fight in single-combat matches."

"And?" She inches her legs apart, an invitation. Behind her, the foreign duelist makes a disgusted noise and climbs out of their bath, then to the dressing parlor.

"And I can get a roster of the applicants, should you wish to …" Yifen's thumbs a warm, oiled line up Nuawa's thigh. "Get preemptive."

"Which ex-partner or enemy do you want gotten rid of?"

"Little cynic. What if I just want you to win and bring Sirapirat the glory we've long been denied, even though we produce fighters as fit as any for the army?"

Nuawa slides into one of the pools, down until the water comes up to her throat then her face. Her hair flares in naga corona, snake-tendrils floating in the water. She shuts her eyes, feels the grime of perspiration and leopard-carried grudge sluice away. When she emerges, she finds Yifen laid flat against the floor, chin in hands and watching with undisguised interest. The gaze of a hawk on prey.

Nuawa wipes hot water from her mouth. "Are you not participating, then, in this tournament of tournaments?"

"Given what'll happen to the losers? I'd rather not." Yifen cards her fingers through Nuawa's drenched hair, tickling an earlobe. "The soldier's life is not for me, besides. Too demanding and I'd look terrible in that uniform. You, though, have just the right mindset and could go far. Only don't forget me when you rise high in the general's favor, hmm?"

"You overestimate me," Nuawa murmurs. The pool is churning, curse-vestiges calling out hungry ghosts from the pipes. She climbs out. "But tell me more and I'll do my best."

Out in the streets, away from the luxuries of the Marrow, Sirapirat is bitterly cold.

Nuawa's boots crunch on new snow, her hands and body all but disappearing into the bulk of her coat and gloves and furs. Her breath curls in the air, the warmth of the bath already a distant dream. Mother tells her that Sirapirat once knew three seasons. Hot, wet, cool. Monsoons and storms, draughts and floods, rice paddies running full and mangoes bursting on the tongue. *It is beautiful at first, snow,* Mother would say, *until it erases and turns all you know into a copy of itself. Soon you no longer recall a time without; soon you forget warmth and buffaloes dozing by the river-bank. Soon, you remember only what it wants you to remember.*

She can't picture any of that and has never seen a live buffalo, though there are paintings and sculptures in galleries, in museums. The queen doesn't forbid commemoration of the past, regards them with the apathy most might regard an insect— inconsequential, beneath her notice. No museum in the world, no shelf of gold-leaf history and marble maps, can alter the absoluteness of winter. The only thing the queen forbids is fire. Candles and lamps are allowed, barely; pyres are prohibited outright. Cremation used to be the truest form of bidding the dead farewell and seeing them off into the rebirth cycle. Now they are consigned to the queen's machines that turn them into power that warms, feeds, and animates Sirapirat's infrastructure.

Fifty years winter has reigned over Sirapirat, out of Mother Indrahi's sixty. Fifty out of the seventy Nuawa's giving-mother Tafari would have been, if she were alive today.

Nuawa cranes her neck back, gazing up at the sky where

Sirapirat's second self resides. Up there Sirapirat is vivid with color, golden spires and scriptoriums, silver palaces and lapis gardens. Yet even there, the mirage said to have been painted as Sirapirat's ideal self, the gardens glitter with frost. Mother's fruits do not bud on the branches, mangoes and mangosteens absent. Jasmines and globe amaranths do not bloom on the bushes. Instead, the phantom trees are coated in snow, their boughs bare and bleached.

Along the streets, she occasionally spots a likeness of herself on laminated boards, a distant likeness with rather more height and bosom than the reality, eyelids and cheeks and lips painted to hyperreal emphasis. But most recently the foreigner gets more play on the Marrow's advertisements, being exotic and newer. She stops to watch an imprint of her latest match. It replays, over and over, the part where she chops the heads off the leopards—four decisive swings, four decisive decapitations. *Nuawa of the Lightning.* A moniker she's always disliked but which Tezem insists upon. Improbably, it's caught on.

Her home is perched on the hills of Matiya Street, a neighborhood of tenements housing students, non-tenured professors, various researchers and academics of the less-prestigious stratum. The Marrow offers lodgings to a duelist of her caliber, but she prefers distance between home and work. Her apartment is better-furnished than most, vintage rather than run-down, a double façade of wood reinforced by steel. Octagonal windowpanes and pots of white cyclamens blushing magenta. A spirit shrine on the highest balcony, visible from the ground, laden with tiny dishes of condiments and baked rice. The landlady, like Nuawa's mother, belongs to a generation that recalls the time before winter, a generation that takes her faith seriously.

She unlocks her room with a jade key. Her mother helped decorate and accordingly the ceiling is busy with meshes of rough bismuth and amethyst for luck, the chimes depending from them tinkling as Nuawa enters. She inhales the heat and sheds her coat, gloves, tightly laced boots. Heating—like water, like so much else—is ever powered by ghosts. Justice in Sirapirat has become much hungrier since winter's advent. Large thefts send the convicted to the kilns much oftener than to a prison sentence or rehabilitation among the monks. Even then much of the city goes cold and hungry; production of ghosts does not match the demand, especially when a portion is taxed for the queen's vaults.

She wrings the meltwater from her hair and checks on her cyclamens. In good shape. Thinking of her mother, she breathes on her calling-glass.

Indrahi answers, face appearing in hazy reflection. Behind her, there is a diptych of a summer sky: a blue so deep, a sun so bright, the leaves gigantic and the flowers riotous. She is doing beadwork in her lap, a complicated tangle of soft wire and semi-precious stones. Next to her, a bowl of persimmons sliced crescent and fine as a moon in wane. "Nuawa," Mother says. "How does it go? I've watched some of your recent fights."

Unlike her brother—who fled for ordainment as soon as he could, taking on the saffron robe—Mother never cautions or chides her for her profession; if anything has encouraged it. *I want a child who can defend herself and what she loves. There is a time for piety, for pacifism, but we are at war.* "The latest was leopards. Maybe they wanted a novelty to cap off the season."

"Very symbolic."

They chat, Nuawa asking after her mother's arboretum, Indrahi inquiring whether the landlady has kept up good maintenance and whether Nuawa is taking up more contract work. There is always demand for bodyguards who have done well at the Marrow. Then the subject veers to the tribute tournament, and Nuawa asks, "Mother, what do you know about the queen's general?"

"Lussadh al-Kattan." Indrahi cocks her head. "I've studied

her. A dangerous person and an unnatural child, all that troubled history. What of her?"

"The tribute game. Our first."

"Ah." Her mother nods slowly; evidently she too has heard the particulars. "The prize is real. One of their new officers was selected this way from a tribute game in Jalsasskar, three months past. And thus, so many fools will enter this one, hoping— praying—to be the next; sure that they have the prowess and the luck. The queen is excellent at tricking us into feeding ourselves to the kiln."

"Am I a fool, Mother?"

Indrahi puts down the beadwork and laughs. "I raised you better than that."

To lose is to go into the ghost kiln, a forever poltergeist. "Then may I have your leave to join the game?"

Her mother stops laughing. But she does not admonish; she does not disallow. Instead she says, "Then I will tell you all I know of the queen's general. First you must know this, the most important: if the queen can be said to have a heart, then she has given that heart into the keeping of General Lussadh al-Kattan."

TWO

THE NIGHT TRAIN SLIDES INTO THE ENCLOSURE WITH THE smoothness of a hand into glove, barely juddering, a harmony of engine-parts and a hundred ghosts working in unison. The platform is nearly empty this close to midnight, a handful of vendors peddling the last of their roasted sweet potatoes, glutinous rice, gamey meat harvested from city birds. A stray dog curls up for warmth, some mongrel creature with the musculature of a hunting hound and the thick coat of a cattle herder. Lussadh steps past it, past the vendors, pulling her coat up around her neck and winding her scarf around her head. She is alone.

It is not the first time she has been to Sirapirat, though she doesn't visit often, this remote and provincial territory. She is familiar with the layout, has made a point of studying its map as she makes the point of studying every major constituent. Difficult to get lost, in any case. The palace is visible from the train station, uphill and wide, a layered compound of curlicued roofs and steep paths. Stairs that run spirals, as if to test the endurance and will of supplicants. The gold mirage limns the streets and roofs and storm drains even at night, upside down and ever vigilant, as though waiting for the reality below to transfigure into a reflection of above. Even the architecture is different, harking to a time when this was a humid, tropical region. More wood than stone, airy floors with wide windows, absent the pipes and arteries that distribute heat. Lussadh imagines what it does to the spirit of the locals to have this constant reminder of the past. Even fifty years down, there are still seditionists.

The mirage admits no stars, barely the moons. Everything gold. Lussadh watches her own shadow pool deep amber, oily and malleable. She passes a group of drunk students, workers returning home from a late shift; none recognize her, as she prefers. A temple is admitting one last petitioner before shutting its gate for the night. Sirapirat is the least nocturnal of any developed territory she has been to, quiet and orderly in late hours as though under curfew.

She reaches the palace on foot, goes through a lesser gate that opens only to her and the queen. None of the sentries notices her, a fault she'll have to take up with their commander later.

Her quarters have been prepared in advance, credit to the Sirapirat servants. As with all other palaces her suite is decorated to the queen's tastes. Not ones that Lussadh herself shares, but she's learned to abide. Pale silks veil the bed and window, filtering the already-thin light into pastel hues. The floor is lacquered ebony, the bed an affair of coral frame and posts growing wild, mattress hard and the sheets a lambent green.

In the middle of the mattress, a dead hummingbird.

It is small, singularly beautiful, the brow purple and the throat turquoise, the breast bright peridot. One leg has been broken off, one wing bent backward to the cusp of *snap*. It couldn't have been easy to procure one of these, a desert hummingbird far from home and once the crest of the al-Kattan dynasty. She takes the dead thing in her palm. The blood has crusted and the body is brittle, weightless. It can't be more than hours old. Whoever planted this knew when she would arrive—

she's kept her exact schedule quiet; Sirapirat staff should know only the approximate date—and picked an interval of time where other palace servants would not see and take it out in time. Unless they have an endless supply of this specific bird. A symbol, in a climate of symbols. Nothing is without significance.

Lussadh wonders whether the culprit thought the repercussions through; that others would be chastised in their stead. Or else that is the point, to provoke her into punishing the entire staff and incite resentment. It doesn't matter that Sirapirat's conquest predated her joining the queen's service by three decades. In the queen's absence, she is as close to the face of winter as there can be.

She wraps the corpse in paper, setting it aside. Then she draws her calling-glass from where it rests next to her heart, and says aloud, "Your Majesty."

A fog of chill, an eddy of snow, and the queen resolves into image. Perfect, just as the real one is, hair moving gently in a breeze of its own, brocade robe indigo against a complexion that is unique to her: tinted by no arteries, faintly luminescent like the sheen of a good opal. "How is Sirapirat? I trust your journey was without event."

"I have arrived safely. Not even a single assassination attempt. So disappointing."

The queen's refraction bends, warps, and joins Lussadh on the edge of the bed. "I see you are alone, unguarded. Do you mean to drive your retinue quite mad with worry? Surely you were not in so much haste to get there."

Lussadh laughs. "I'm not so defenseless as all that, my queen. How goes your talk with the occidental ambassadors? Do they still think we haven't invaded them because they have no fear of the cold?"

"All mammal humors freeze the same. The human body is the most fragile, the most delicate." A phantom hand, part-real, runs along the line of Lussadh's throat. Up, down. "The most exquisite."

The refraction is just that, mirage without heft, but Lussadh leans into that spectral hand all the same. "Already I miss you."

"When we meet again, I'll make you senseless; I'll take you into my mouth until you cry for mercy." The queen kisses her, full on the lips. "I will keep you with me for days, as long as your mortal stamina can last. You'll be raw, everywhere."

Lussadh parts her mouth, but all she feels is a distant chill. The queen does not kiss her like this in person, not after those first two times. One kiss to wake the mirror shard in her heart, two to bind and nourish it. A third carries its own significance, but the queen has never admitted what. She keeps few secrets from Lussadh; this is the foremost, and one which bothers Lussadh more than she would like to admit. She makes herself smile. "You'll make it very difficult to concentrate on my task here. And my bed so empty."

"You are free to fill it, as you desire." An ethereal thumb brushes her earlobe and a hand slides under her jacket, resting at the base of Lussadh's spine; the queen's refraction has a trick of being *more*—present in multiples, before and behind, her reach omnipresent. It invites pleasant, exciting possibilities, were it endowed with more substance. "My empire has grown immense and yet there is but one general. I enjoy the company of many and allow them hope, yet you alone occupy my bed. But you must know that I do not require the same of you, and never will. I want you to sate yourself, have all the fulfillment your flesh can offer."

From anyone else it would imply the opposite, an admonishment, but she's known the queen long enough; what Her Majesty says is exactly what is meant, however roundabout or strange. "Not at the moment. I will start scouting for other bearers tomorrow, though I expect most will have signed up for the games."

Those touched by the queen's mirror always do, drawn to violence in all its forms. Children, adolescent, adult.

The queen's eyes brighten—for her, this is literal: a sudden gleam, as of a candle flaring up behind obsidian. "You are there in my stead, in all ways. You are peerless and I trust wholly in you. Any candidates you find, you must tell me at once."

"Of course, Your Majesty. My life for yours," Lussadh says, the ritual words that are to her more than ritual. "All that I am is for you."

"And as much of myself that I can grant is yours alone."

Another kiss on her brow, and the queen dissolves.

Lussadh sits alone for a long time, hand on her sternum where the glass splinter binding her to the queen resides: greater than any vow, more lasting than any matrimony. She has seen it once when the queen found her and brought the mirror shard to life. It shone inside her, all of her, having spread its capillaries throughout her bones. The queen laughed then—the only time since she saw the queen laugh like that—in giddy delight; it was the first time she began to think of winter's embodiment as human-like. That within the armor, behind the alien face, there was a spirit capable of emotion, even joy.

She has not been able to articulate that her doubt is not in whether she is the queen's sole lover or the queen's one and only general. It is in the knowledge that they have gathered a score of soldiers who harbor pieces of the same mirror as Lussadh, yet the queen has not stopped looking. She has said none of this, will never say any of it. To admit that doubt suppurates in her like a wound is to concede she is weak, and to ask the question outright courts the truth that she *has* failed to satisfy.

Such petty fears that should have been beneath her. How the queen has altered her to the core.

She doesn't sleep much that night; instead she examines the tournament roster and the structure. The first segment will be conducted using oneiric drugs and dream arenas to speed up the process, unconventional but one with promise. She approved it a few months back, though she has yet to meet the oneirologist responsible; recommended by the city's premier arena, the Marrow, and apparently a recluse. Then there is an occidental ambassador awaiting an audience with her, representing one of their central states. Lussadh briefly toys with the idea of delegating that to her lieutenant—once he arrives along with the rest of her entourage—but no: he's too new, not particularly suited. For all that she finds occidental representatives tiring to deal with, even the queen does not shirk that chore. A necessary courtesy. At the present the queen has little interest in the distant continent: a question of scale and supply chain, and moreover the queen says mirror-pieces tend not to attach themselves to occidentals. Incompatibility in spirit, perhaps.

At dawn, she once more covers herself up and steals out of the palace, the dead bird in hand.

Down Matiya Street she looks for the shop she visited five years ago, finds to her surprise that it is still there. The front window displays mounted buffalo heads, taxidermied owls, an assortment of small animals. The doorbell rings noisily as she enters, a cascade of brass chimes. A thick smell of preservatives and musk; the place evidently does not ventilate well, and there are no windows. She spots the proprietor in the back. "Ziya," she calls.

Ziya Jiang looks up from a shelf—incongruously—of ammunition boxes. "General! I knew you'd be here for the games, but not that you'd visit my humble business. How staggering to be in your presence once more." He limps toward her, bowing. A bad leg sustained in battle while under her command one decade ago. "What do you require?"

"I'll need this put into some kind of shape. As alive as you can make it look." She puts the dead bird on the counter. "I'll pay upfront."

"Certainly not, General. Hah, I see what this is. Pretty. How *are* you, sir?"

"Missing one of my best tacticians." Lussadh nods toward the back shelves; a few firearms are on display, artisan models. Mostly pistols, the odd rifle. "How did you develop a clientele so eclectic, anyway? Taxidermy and guns."

"I also sell living pets," Ziya says, waving a hand, "just not here. Business friends always tell me to diversify, so I do. I hear you had to put down insurgents in Kavaphat a couple months back?"

"Religious fanatics. Nothing special." Surprisingly well-armed and disciplined, in truth, and gifted with local support. She glances at a pistol with a sanded-metal handgrip, the barrel made of some dark alloy striated in silver capillaries. Like the rest, it looks custom-made. "Is that for sale?"

"I'm afraid not. The grip would be too small for your hand, General; it was tailored for one of my clients. This gunsmith is rather exclusive, but if you'd like one similar I can try to persuade. Very versatile piece, works with most unconventional rounds. Ah—I think that's my client here to pick it up."

Lussadh retreats to the back of the shop, watching a person push through the door, another jangle of chimes—she supposes Ziya wants plenty of notice. The person is in their thirties, difficult to tell whether south or north of it; they have the look of a Sirapirat native, a smoothness of appearance that makes age interminable. Sleek shoulder-length hair, average build under the thick coat, and moves like a trained combatant; someone who knows hand-to-hand. An interesting face, features built as though for calligraphy, bold brushstrokes for mouth and eyebrows, a narrow straight nose.

The person—a woman, going by how Ziya addresses her— handles the gun, testing its weight. Her gaze turns toward Lussadh; she is not unaware there is another customer present. A few seconds of appraisal before she turns back to Ziya, making a perfunctory effort at haggling.

"Who was that?" Lussadh asks after the stranger has paid and gone. A mix of curiosity and something else. She recognizes this for what it is—this is how it begins when she comes across another of her kind, those holding a fragment of the queen's mirror.

"A duelist at the Marrow. Semi-famous, decently successful." Ziya scribbles a figure down in his ledger. "I taught her marksmanship, though that was a while ago."

Her intuition is not infallible, has produced false positives; the body's caprices are easy to confuse with that tug of affinity. The senses fool themselves, muddling the intellect. She would need more time in the woman's company, physical contact, to be sure. "I see," she says. "Can you have the bird ready in a day or two?"

Lussadh's retinue arrives in the evening, bringing with them her luggage, her security detail, and her aide Ulamat. "The queen will have all our heads if she knows we let you travel alone, my lord," he says as he joins her for dinner.

"She'll do no such thing. You're hard to replace. What's my schedule like?"

"The ambassador tomorrow morning. Inspecting the palace in the afternoon; Governor Imnesh will want to meet you, *At the general's convenience of course and no sooner*, as he said." Ulamat's voice takes on a snotty note, mimicking Imnesh. "After that you are free to wander alone and endanger yourself as usual, lord."

"Come now," she says, "have I ever gotten killed? Try the dishes. Apparently their cook isn't half-bad."

The food is a thick curry of lamb, milk curds, and snake shallots; flatbread pearled with black sesame and vermillion garlic;

fried balls made from ground lizard meat and chili pepper, drenched in sauce. Ulamat examines each dish, frowning, taking a taste of each. "Too little garlic, but passable." Kemiraj fare used to be rare in foreign states. After Lussadh became general, chefs across winter territories have been scrambling to learn. Fine dining has been redefined to her tastes, or an approximation of it.

She tears the flatbread into precise pieces. More garlic, as Ulamat says, would have been better, but it is a good effort. The curry is rich and buttery, just the way she likes it. She has argued with Ulamat many times that he is too valuable to be her taster—and in any case the queen's gift keeps her safer than most—but he continues to insist. Adhesive to traditions, and to him she will always be his liege lord, more than even the queen.

He eats like an aristocrat now, after years of coaching, as much removed from the orphan she salvaged from the streets as she is removed from the imperial prince she used to be. Twenty-seven years. In the grand scheme of things, not that long. "Remind me," she says between sips of cicada liquor, "how old are you this year, Ulamat?"

"Thirty-five, though I can never be too sure."

"I worry that you haven't made a life of your own. Marry. Have a child or three."

"No spouse compels me better than duty to you, lord." He helps himself to a large chunk of flatbread. "Unless of course my lord has no more use of her aide."

"I won't be able to do without you any time soon," she says. "Nevertheless, you know perfectly well what I mean. You can have your own life and serve me. It's not mutually exclusive."

Ulamat considers the table, then the plates, then meets her gaze. "I'm not the marrying type, my lord. Let us say that I didn't have much of a model household to learn from. But moreover, I intend to die in your service."

She thinks of the child from back then, at the time to her merely a gesture to show that the throne treated his tribe—children of the enamel—as equally as the rest of its citizens. The studied charity of the king-in-waiting, part of the performance. She'd neglected him at first, leaving him to palace servants to feed and bathe and clothe. Winter was not yet ascendant then, far from a threat to Kemiraj.

"I didn't save you simply for you to die young." When she'd found him, he was malnourished, filthy, and dying from necrotizing wounds. Beaten by other children and his elders. Neither of them would have imagined he would have grown into a man at ease with finery and plenty, fastidious with food, not only literate but erudite. Her mouth twitches. "What a long, strange way we've come."

"I'll try to die of old age, my lord, but that's contingent on you taking better care of yourself."

And if pressed, Lussadh supposes, she would say that she lives to die in the queen's service. On it goes, a chain of self-sacrifice, stopping at Her Majesty who exists for herself alone. "Very well. Let us drink to the durability of that which we bind ourselves to. Absolute winter."

Ulamat hefts his glass. "To your everlasting victory."

She follows suit. "To the queen's eternal reign."

THREE

Nuawa comes across a medallion bearing a likeness of the general's grandaunt in Tezem's collection. She must have seen it before, but has never had a reason to pay it any special heed, just another unremarkable object eclipsed by much more unusual curiosities.

Her manager's office apes the aesthetic of an antique shop, full shelves and cabinets, preserved paintings and outdated maps on the walls. Most of them are exotic: there is a miniature greenhouse that holds live flora cycling through the seasons that once were, budding green and fruiting the bright shades of summer — ruby lychees and quartz rose apples, amber carambolas and golden papayas. Tezem boasts that the tiny things, no larger than Nuawa's fingernail, can be extracted with delicate tweezers and needles to eat. That is a treat they reserve for special guests and the most exceptional duelists. Nuawa took some home once for her mother.

At the sight of them, Indrahi wept; it was the only time Nuawa had seen her mother cry. The reminder of seasons that were, the fruits themselves. She couldn't tell and did not ask.

Her manager has not emerged yet, though their appointment

has gone fifteen minutes past. Nuawa knows Tezem too well to knock on the small door to their private study. Instead she waits by the miniature aquarium, another expensive curio and toy, in which the waters thresh bathyal green; tiny shadow-carps dart through the darkness, flashing black-light fins and starlit eyes.

Compared to them the medallion is ordinary, out of place in its mundanity. A flat disc of some pale metal that has not oxidized, circumscribed with a script Nuawa can't read but recognizes as the Kemiraj alphabet. The face resembles General Lussadh's only in passing, but the familial tie is visible if one looks for it. Harsh cheekbones, prominent philtrum, angle of the eyes: the king of Kemiraj before winter took it. Lussadh—prince back then—would have been the next in line, chosen as successor for her gift at statecraft and languages.

Instead, Prince Lussadh had struck a bargain with the Winter Queen in secret: she would surrender in Kemiraj's name, and in exchange she would not only be spared but granted favor with the queen. The entire dynasty was slaughtered. No al-Kattan survives save Lussadh herself—not her grandaunt, not her siblings, not her parents.

An unnatural child, Mother said, and Nuawa is inclined to agree. She has killed her share of opponents in duels and more besides in contract work; she feels no remorse for it, but this gives even her pause. She can't begin to model a mind capable of that. Even the queen is easier to conceptualize—alien and there-fore logical in her inhumanity. At least she has not, to Nuawa's knowledge, committed fratricide.

By the time Tezem deigns to present themselves, Nuawa is seated primly in a chair that has escaped colonization by unusual instruments or amber-encased manuscripts, well away from the medallion or anything else. She has disassembled one of her knives: its fishbone ribs cling like angular lace to the back of her hand, twitching, as she cleans out its core with a pin.

"I hate it when you do that," they say as they relocate a pile of books, freeing a divan for themselves.

"Someone's shadow got stuck in it. I don't want it to congeal." Nuawa flicks out a shred of void. "Good morning, Tezem."

"You are here to discuss signing up for the tribute game, aren't you?"

She re-binds the sliver-knife and sheathes it. "Do you object?"

Tezem crosses their legs. Their eyes are painted metallic, courting ocean colors, and underscored with kohl. Austere clothes, in deliberate contrast. Tezem enjoys dressing in opposites. "You're one of the best ten duelists in Sirapirat."

"One of the best five, I'd prefer to think."

"The competition involves three hundred participants. By the deadline, that'll have swollen to four hundred if not more. That is a great deal of unknown variables. Fifty Sirapirat duelists? That I'll bet on. Gods know how many foreigners? That's a different set of odds entirely."

She knows from Yifen that most tribute participants are not from Sirapirat, but rather from adjacent constituents. Those who did not make it in the qualification preliminaries there, those who survived defeat—without being fed to the ghost-kiln—through some escape clause. No doubt they believe Sirapirat fighters to be of an inferior grade, that they'll have an easier time here. "I appreciate your concern. Life is nothing but unknown variables."

"You're determined then." Tezem gives a long, theatrical sigh. "My best-earning duelist gone to a ghost. Truly I'll miss you. Well, my ledgers will miss you. Do you reckon I could write you off as a tax deduction?"

"Very touched. You'll need to ask your accountant." Nuawa makes a show of examining her fingernails. "Or you could consider this an investment. Put me in the game; I understand a reputable manager can get me in this late without me having to jump through hoops. A number of the foreign competitors are fugitives. Sirapirat law enforcement doesn't apply to them — wrong jurisdiction — and if they succeed in the tournament, they'll be pardoned fully. Until the game begins properly though, the original bounties on their heads stand."

Tezem taps the divan's armrest with a steel-tipped fingernail. "What's in it for me? I won't get into this just for sentiment's sake, you must realize."

"The bounties I can't collect without going through bureaucrats and I expect you can take care of that, so every last coin made from that is yours. My presence in the tournament will attract new clients for you. What have you got to lose?"

They look at her, frowning. "I'll get you a list of the fugitives," they say at length. "You get until the hard deadline to put them out of commission. Then and only then will I sponsor you into the tournament."

The hard deadline being in six days. "It's a deal," Nuawa says, already calculating the logistics of each coming kill.

The alacrity with which Tezem secured enforcer documents is this side of divine intervention: profit motivates them, as ever, to sharp immediacy. Nuawa receives the warrants in the form of temporary tattoos that she presses over her shoulder. They bind to her blood, granting her legal authority from six different provinces to act on eight separate bounties. Eight in six days: cutting it close, but not impossible. She's faced tougher contract work when money was tight, before she came into the comfort of the Marrow.

Her first pick is an occidental who immigrated to marry his husband. Apparently the husband cheated and, in a fit of pique, the occidental set a building on fire. The prize on his head is not high, but neither is his low-rent room secured. Simple enough to slip in and wait. She skimps on ammunition, opting to take him with a blade.

It is quick business and he falls almost before he realizes there's an intruder in his room. Confirming the kill is the messier part: she has to carve out the man's heart—not for the first time she's glad she keeps her knives whetted and well-fed—and daub blood on the warrant. That tattoo turns warm, nearly scalding, before it evaporates and takes the blood with it. Nuawa leaves the body and the heart; both seep fluids into the rough floor. She doesn't envy the janitor or landlady, but neither does she wish to bother with corpse disposal.

By the fourth day, she has gone through six bounties.

She is waiting for her seventh in the university's library. An odd shelter, but rooming with a professor offers somewhat better protection than the previous six, who all lived in isolated apartments. Nuawa blends in with ease: she's too old for an undergraduate, but she has no trouble affecting the harried look of a postgraduate or academic staff. Her profile gives no hint of hidden weapons. A smoothness of line aided by clever cutting in her clothes and her practice at carrying concealed. Nuawa puts a great deal of value on good tailors, invests much of her earnings into them. She's also put aside all the accoutrements of a duelist, the customary accessorizing of enemy signatures as trophy: no spent bullets button her shirt, no pearl molars embroider her throat, and no chips of shattered blades glitter in her hair. Amidst the stacks and dragonfly papers, ink-stained and tousled as any student, she waits and watches with a book before her. Now and again she squints at its marginalia and copies it onto a sheet of folding resin.

She hears the quiet in gradients, in ripples—conversations extinguishing, pens stilling, amber pebbles juddering to a stop on abacuses. A thump of books dropping on tabletops, a thud of writing slates falling to the stone floor. Their sequels: papers scattering, record-panes shattering. In a moment, the only sound is General Lussadh's steps, and those of her companion.

Nuawa forces herself to calm, her rhythms to even out. Her entire family has changed their names, scattered far from Sirapi-rat, and most have already disowned her mothers. And when Tafari died in the kiln, the general was still a prince. Lussadh would never have met Tafari.

"My apologies, esteemed scholars; it wasn't my intent to disrupt." Said with perfect courtesy. "I'm showing my guest around the university, though I *should* have notified your superiors beforehand, shouldn't I? Send the costs for damage I caused to the palace steward and I'll see that you're properly reimbursed."

Behind her rampart of papers and manuscripts, Nuawa studies the general. She has seen Lussadh before in broadcasts, never in person. The queen's right hand is broad-shouldered and tall, superbly made and at forty-six superbly fit. Immense eyes that might have been called limpid on a younger, less severe face. The jawline is aggressive, the angle of chin and nose definite. The whole is striking, even handsome. Appealing if not for the mind behind it, the allegiance it is yoked to. And oddly familiar, in a way she can't quite place.

Their eyes meet, for the push-pull of a heartbeat.

The general leaves with her companion—a young occidental woman, like some diplomat—to their business, and soon Nuawa leaves to hers.

By the time she is done, her seventh bounty is a pile of ashes and dissipating shadow. A few smoke talismans help her dispose of the corpse, more or less neatly. Blots of gore linger on her clothes, result of too much struggle and resistance. She covers them up with her jacket, longing for hot baths.

On the way out, she turns to the library, knowing that a hasty exit would mark her. Not that collecting the bounty is criminal, but she prefers to make no scene. Seven down, one to go. She takes no pride in the kill but she does take pride in the efficiency.

By now the library is empty except for the general. Who has been here for some time, Nuawa supposes, and whose presence has chased out students or professors alike. The occidental woman is gone.

Nuawa takes her time with the books, browsing the shelves, taking out and putting back volumes on ancient textiles, orthogonal warfare, swamp ecology. Subjects of incredible specialization, and which have been subjected to incredible organization. The university has an exacting library system. In the end she takes a volume on lapidary, heavy and plated. Holding it to her chest, she joins the general. "Glory to you, General, and to the grace of winter absolute." There was a time, young and full of ideal, when those words would have stung her tongue and stoppered her throat. No longer; now they are rote. Existence is a performance.

"An interesting choice of reading."

"The illustrations are beautiful," Nuawa says, and they are. Brilliant inks, intense as jewels or scarab wings, primary colors and bold lines. "I don't see them often."

"Actual butterflies? No, one wouldn't. They are not insects built to survive, too specialized. Fragile, but I'll agree that they are beautiful." Up close, Lussadh looms, with or without meaning to. The Kemiraj are statuesque, their royals even more so. She wears a faint scent, some subtle myrrh. "A moment of your time, if I might?"

Said with the surety that *no* is not an answer any sane person will give. "It would be my honor to give the general my time, though it is as of little worth as rubble next to a pearl."

"In most circumstances, rubble is of more practical use. Paperweights. Burials. Their uses are infinite, but pearls have just the one, and not even an interesting one at that." The general takes her elbow, a courteous gesture, but the grip is firm.

Her pulse beating copper percussion in her throat, Nuawa follows the general into a reading room. A plain oblong table; five chairs, two stacked with a student's forgotten assignments; a wide clear window, full of dusk and lake. Rimed, with frost lotuses floating blue and serene. No tadpoles, fish, waterstriders. Aquatic life native to Sirapirat were never meant for the cold. Humankind alone adapts, if only just. Indrahi would tell her, when she was little, of all the infants succumbing before Sirapirat surrendered and was granted ghost-heat.

Lussadh does not block the door, but she does pick the chair closest to it. Gesticulates. "Next to me." Nuawa complies. "You smell of blood and smoke. Somehow those don't seem like a combination the biology faculty would produce."

Giving her a chance to wriggle on the interrogation hook. "Perhaps I work at an abattoir, General, or the kitchen." She's careful to lace this with irony, edge it with a half-smile, to show that she is not saying it seriously—that having nothing to hide, she needs not lie or make excuses. That all she is doing is fencing.

"An abattoir where they smoke the meat in-house and their employees leave with pristine clothes? A kitchen where the cooks keep their hair this neat and don't smell at all of lard or condiments?" The corners of Lussadh's mouth edge upward, trajectory following Nuawa's. The general too accepts that this is a pretense, a joke. "You are not the kind of danger I expect to encounter at an institution of learning. Here one expects the bureaucrat's hazard, the academic's tenure failure, not a killer. Are you here to remove me? It's been too long since the last attempt and I've grown indolent."

Still the edge of a jest, veering toward not quite. "There's no one alive more dangerous than you, General." Nuawa keeps her voice and face bland, composed: it is not flattery she means to give, nor obsequiousness she means to project. From what Indrahi said, the general enjoys neither.

"I can think of a few things. A pack of wild wolves, uncontrolled weather, fate's vagaries. I am but one person." Lussadh drums her knuckles against the tabletop, frowning. Her fingers still, as though she's reached a decision. "I'm about to do something indecorous and ask that you not hold it against me. It's not out of lust or malice."

Nuawa has time to tense—brace herself to dodge, to counterattack—before Lussadh leans in. The general's mouth on hers is so abrupt and so *improbable* that her senses blank out. When they return to function, it is a rush: the roughness of a scar on the general's philtrum, the contrasting softness of the general's lips, the pressure of the general's hand on her jaw. And then the tug on her nerves, almost physical, ice that at once burns and chills her arteries.

Lussadh draws away. Runs her tongue along her own mouth, tasting Nuawa. "Carrying concealed is all very well, but it does show. Of course, I do know what to look for and I've perhaps gotten much closer to you than most. You're a fighter of some kind, correct?"

Dazed, Nuawa says without thinking, "Yes."

"Good. I hope to see you at the tribute tournament. May I have your name? Mine you already know, more's the pity. Everyone has the advantage of me."

"Nuawa Dasaret." And saying that she snaps back to herself, caught by the mortification of having answered so simply and truthfully. But then, if Lussadh wants to find out more about her, the general has plenty of channels. Lying about her name—a name far disconnected from her giving-mother, from Tafari's history—would serve her poorly. And her original name is, after all, dead. A child, six-year-old, buried under granite and soil.

"A hypnotic name." The general smiles, a flash of well-kept teeth, and makes a gallant bow. "I'll remember it."

FOUR

NIGHT. WIND SLICES ACROSS LUSSADH'S NECK, GARROTE-
sharp, and she wakes. A gun in her hand even before she regis-
ters the parted window: so much life and habit have taught her,
honing this reflex until it is as natural as blinking. The curtain
flutters and in the distance, an owl hoots. She's come to think of
owls as an everywhere animal, canny at surviving in all weather
and habitats. Even at home, so long ago, her grandaunt kept
several pet owls. A symbol of resilience and cunning. If not for
tradition, her grandaunt would have abandoned the hummingbird for an owl, something dark and wide of wings. Something
with beaks designed to tear open meat.

There is no movement. She is alone, despite the evidence of
entry. Slowly she shrugs off the furs and strains to see, to listen,
but the rime cobwebs overhead are undisturbed and the frost-
spiders quiescent: a gift from the queen to keep watch over her
better than any human guard, as much alarm system as the first
line of defense. Capable of reducing a person to bones in
minutes.

"Your Highness." The voice is the crackle of wood wilting in fire, of sand-waves lapping at a dune and desert sails snapping in the wind. The voice is one that belongs to another lifetime.

And so she says, with difficulty, "That was a country ago, Ytoba, and a title that no longer exists."

"Blood is forever. To me you will always be of your dynasty, and your children thereafter should you spread your seed." A pause. The shadow does not move: it is so thin and flat against the wall it could be paper, monodimensional, not a person at all but a memory and a grudge. "No doubt you thought me dead. I was close to it and my recovery was long. What you meted out to me would have been the death of most. Strange to nearly die by fire given who your new master is."

She attempts to imagine what Ytoba looks like now, shrouded in scraps of gloom and cradled in the interstices between light. Back then, a nation ago, ey was whole and strong and one of Kemiraj's best assassins. Pledged for life to the crown. "You're hardy, as ever."

"I'm less than I used to be, but I'm surprised you didn't make sure I was burned to the bone; that you didn't stay to see my carcass turn to ashes. Did sentiment stay your hand? I've followed your rise."

Lussadh evaluates her response, her exits. She can't shoot at a target which is not entirely corporeal: not the right gun, not the right ammunition. Any help she summons will come too late. Even the queen will not be in time. "I am what I am."

There is hesitation, a ripple in Ytoba's silhouette. "You upended everything. Why did you choose as you did?"

"Framing it as a choice surely misses the point. Think back to where we were, Ytoba. Could Kemiraj have triumphed as the very land turned against us and the sky froze over; as our children and elderly fell? Could you have struck down the Winter Queen?"

"You ask these questions to serve and justify yourself, my prince."

"Some questions must be asked, some decisions made, some actions taken. Chastise me," Lussadh says quietly, "but you didn't make those decisions then. And you were not able to take down the queen. Your one duty and you could not fulfill it. It fell to me to do what had to be done, while sparing as many lives as I could."

No response. But there is a gradual fading, a change in air pressure. It becomes easier, turn by marginal turn, to breathe.

When ey is gone—it is not over but it is a night survived, an encounter circumvented—she shuts the window and for a time presses her brow to the pane, eyes shut, thinking of nothing. Listening to her heartbeat.

The furs have cooled in her absence; it's been close to a year since she last had someone to keep a bed warm. The lack is not difficult to rectify, but she misses decent pillow talk, interesting companionship, something that extends past the act. Courtiers are too naked in their ambition and flattery, courtesans too simplistic in their transaction, and other glass-bearers too jealous of the queen's favor.

Which brings her to her find. Lussadh has never been so sure, so absolute, that she's located another glass-bearer. In Ziya's shop it was a thin intuition; at the university library, it was a confirmation beyond doubt. More strongly than she's ever felt, even with other active glass-bearers already sworn to winter. She could well forego the formality of the tournament and bring Nuawa Dasaret directly to the queen. But first, a background check.

Despite the hour, Ulamat is prompt. He reports to her in the suite's parlor disheveled but alert, as if he'd gone to bed just minutes past. She points to the sideboard, which she's filled with her own liquor and teas. "Make yourself something warm. This will take a while. Do you have anyone on the ground here?"

He sets the water to boil and unlocks the sideboard; everything edible she's brought is well secured, short of breaking the cabinet open. Foodstuff is easy to tamper with, an old lesson from royal life. "The place was a seedbed of strife and radicals. I would fire myself if I had nobody there. What will you require?"

The problem of Ytoba, she decides, will need to wait or at least will require a different instrument. She does not want to risk him until she has a better handle on the old assassin. Ytoba represents all the wrongs that Kemiraj inflicted on the children of the enamel, on Ulamat's people. He would be reckless. Safer, then: "A gladiator named Nuawa Dasaret."

"Ah. Nuawa of the Lightning Flash? Career duelist, my lord. Quite successful, actually; she's been doing this since she was seventeen, a prodigy." He reaches for scrap paper and a pencil, makes a quick sketch. From memory; his is eidetic. "This is what she usually looks like on advertising boards, though the actual person is quite different."

The figure is tall, full-bosomed and wasp-waisted, nose sharp and face upturned to the sky while her hair flares radiant as a sable sun. Her blade, apparently carved from obsidian and impractically enormous, is thrust into a foe's mangled corpse. Lussadh compares the advertisement to the real thing, the woman whose lips taste faintly of salt. Plain, if anything, though those are very soft lips. She imagines them elsewhere. "Slighter of breasts, for one. More muscle, certainly. The illustration does her no justice."

"You've met the Lightning?" Ulamat sets down the cup he's sanitizing, eyes slightly wide.

"You're a fan?" Lussadh laughs. "I know you follow gladiator broadcasts, but isn't Sirapirat a little too backwater? Their duelists can't be that noteworthy."

"They might surprise you. Well—she might surprise you. I've got the name of her manager and should be able to get you information on her family, associates, and history by tomorrow."

Dependable, as ever. "Do check in with Ziya Jiang, an old tutor of hers."

After he is gone, she leans back and wishes he could have produced a dossier on command, that it was already at her desk. Routine work occupies her mind, insulates her from the past. She considers sending out personnel to comb the city for Ytoba, but that is panic speaking: a Kemiraj assassin who doesn't want to be found is like a grain of sand in the desert. There are ways to flush em out and she will think of them once fear recedes and the twisting in her chest stops.

It's been a long time since terror seized her in its jaws with such appetite, so voracious it manifests as physical pressure. The mirror fragments shield each bearer from the excess of human weakness, slowing down fear, fury, grief. Liberating the intellect. It is one of the reasons she accepted the bargain, that first kiss.

Still it does not do away with passion and emotion entirely. It does not negate all injury.

Lussadh dresses and arms herself. Her guard, the newest glass-bearer, starts to attention as she leaves her suite. She waves him aside, not chiding him for failing to notice that there was an assassin in her room: her history is hers alone, at most shared with Ulamat, and in any case Ytoba is not the kind of infiltrator most will detect.

Once the Sirapirat palace was house to a complicated government, part monkhood and part elected officials, a lattice-work of bureaus and divisions. Like most buildings in Sirapirat it was never constructed for cold; one of the first things they had to do was overhaul infrastructure and architecture to accommodate the ghosts. Transport, power, heating. The native ones functioned poorly under winter, as the systems of most annexed constituents tend to. Made for the wrong climate, under the wrong school of thought. Even Kemiraj was like that.

The hallway lamps are dimmed for the night, their radiance slicing shadows into isosceles and trapezoids. She makes a game of evading the sentries. No real challenge since she knows their routes after the inspection, but it's a good test of the local officers. One comes close to spotting her as she nears the engine-shrine. She will need to have another word with their commander.

The further she goes into the old wing, the more of the palace's original self she finds. Colored glass, pieced into tableaus of myth and hunts, catch the light: women with golden wings and crowns of fire, hunting dwarfed humans in a forest. Many-armed gods whose hands end in weapons and mandibles climb fully formed from red lotuses. Ancient style and shadow conspire to make the faces seem hostile to Lussadh, their alien eyes tracking her as she passes.

The door to Vahatma is guarded by viper locks, serpent curlicues whose fangs drip venom in slow, clear beads. Lussadh clicks her tongue and makes staccato claps, timed to a specific rhyme; the serpents unlatch, falling into limp hibernation.

Within is the core of former Sirapirat, captured in the shape of a dualist god. Vahatma. One of its faces is beatific and unpainted, eyes shut in saintly calm. The other is burnished bronze, cheeks stark crimson, mouth an open gash full of filed teeth. A leopard rears in its lap. Two aspects, as Lussadh understands it: peace and war, serenity and wrath, a number of other opposites. Of all the systems native to Sirapirat, this alone functioned until the end. Would have continued to function if the queen's mathematicians had not disabled it.

She runs her hand down its cool, wood-metal waist. A singularly exquisite work of art and, once, the beating heart of Sirapirat's defense. When active, it drew a wall around the city, a high circle of impenetrable shell and concentric lashing teeth. The queen lost a fifth of her army that day, battalions shredded to ribbons of flesh and smears of gore, regiments trapped inside Sirapirat and slaughtered. A fearsome defense: Lussadh has spoken to the handful of retired veterans who survived that fight, and they described Sirapirat's shield as more monster—or a force of nature—than a simple wall, a simple artifice.

Perversely, she would have liked to see it in action for herself. But all she has are portraits, descriptions, memoirs of trauma and terror. The victory afterward did not erase the nightmares of those who survived. The queen ordered an immediate retreat after Vahatma's deployment. In any normal skirmish, the shield would have been decisive. But the queen was patient and her weapon was the land itself, the sky, the winds. If the climate around Sirapirat taxed even her, if the heat and monsoons resisted her, it succumbed in the end. She alone sufficed for a siege, and Sirapirat needed to eat. Its people required heat — their first winter, at war, was a lethal one. Once the wall fell at last, Her Majesty had the god-engine eviscerated, its innards ripped out and preserved in one of her secret vaults. Even Lussadh has no idea where those parts are held. All that remains is this beautiful shell.

But Sirapirat's citizens live well now, granted access to greater comforts and conveniences than they ever had before. "And my grandaunt's subjects live under fairer terms," she says to a dark corner where Ytoba might inhabit. "They live more justly. There are no more inheritances of power, of wealth born into. Before winter, all are equal, whether scions of the dynasty or of the enamel. The least laborer's child is given the same education as the most opulent landlord's scion. If you think the queen cruel, still she does not pursue petty power. She will not execute a servant's clan because they spilled milk on her or broke her favorite vase. Do you understand, Ytoba? Life under the Kemiraj throne was fine enough for you, for me. For most of the country, it was a charnel house."

The shadow does not answer. Were Ytoba here, ey would have refuted the argument in any case: that the unnatural frost slaughtered and starved many in the first few years, as it has done in most constituents. That the queen is not the rightful ruler. Any number of retorts and then, finally, a knife in her throat. Ey would be quick about it, grant her an end as painless as can be had.

"The creation of a more just government, a better distribution of mercy, requires a sacrifice." Lussadh steps away from the two-sided god. "That is the eternal truth, the currency of all existence. No threat will sway me from this, old friend, and my death will not undo history nor alter the course of Kemiraj's future."

Even a peerless killer, an impossible phantom, can be captured. That which lives can be bled, and this time she will make certain it is final. A relic of her past, a landmark of her home. The last standing reminder that she was a traitor to her empire.

FIVE

ON THE MORNING OF THE TOURNAMENT PRELIMINARIES, Nuawa leaves her mother's house at dawn. Before she departs, she pays her respects to an icon of Vahatma. Keeping one is not outlawed, but it is not looked favorably upon, a clear signal for suspicion. The shrine is well hidden in her mother's room in the crook of a cabinet: an ignominious place for a god, but needs must. She says a short prayer and leaves a coin.

"I won't be coming back again any time soon," she says to Indrahi, half-apologetic. "Until the tournament ends, and even after that I'm not sure."

"You shouldn't." Her mother kisses her on the cheek, runs one hand quickly over her hair. "Better play it safe, though I'll miss you. I would ask your brother to say a blessing for you, but he is as he is."

Not formally family anymore, and not just because his ordainment requires a severance of ties with the material world. She puts her arms around Indrahi, whose smallness always comes as a shock, slender bones and delicate frame. Her mother has a trick of occupying more space than her body commands, for all that Nuawa's been taller and broader since late puberty.

"Your blessing will more than suffice, Mother. Whenever I can, I'll send couriers."

"I don't need to tell you to be careful. Nevertheless."

"I will be," Nuawa says, "and I will succeed."

She boards a carriage full of students and laborers from nearby farms and orchards. The ride back to the city, an hour and some fifteen minutes, is fragrant with soil and greenhouse.

On her way to the Marrow, she passes an execution. A plaza where, at weekends, pavilions and stalls are raised for a market. Today it is empty and colorless save for this spectacle. The crowd watching is small, mostly gawking foreigners from the occident or the southern islands. One pallid, orange-headed man is furiously sketching the scene, his tongue lolling like a dog's in concentration. No doubt the tableau will be titled something provocative—or at least faux-profound—back in his country.

It doesn't happen often these days, though she supposes Lussadh's arrival has stirred up the embers of old dissidents, the ones who could not resist. There are some twenty, thirty prisoners in all, lined up two by two, flanked and herded by soldiers in frost-iron uniforms. From the outside, the ghost-kiln looks innocuous: the shape of a large, windowless carriage. Plainly made—it flies no banner, bears no sigil, though its ownership and purpose can never be mistaken.

The condemned wear little: thin shirts, shapeless trousers, sarongs that snap in the wind. Their feet are bare too, as though the clothing and boots been set aside for the living, handed over to kith and kin. Where they are going, they won't need it, warmth and wool being expensive. Imported all, sold by traders who can name their prices, less precious only than the treated wax and incenses that feed the ghosts. Nuawa has known neighbors who volunteered to be fed so their family could afford a few more ghosts, eat slightly better, attend the university. Volunteers get a fair recompense, insofar as a life can be measured by ledgers. Young or old, healthy or sick, the variables don't matter. In the kiln, all are equal.

She idly speculates what these convicts have committed or at least been accused of. Distributed seditious literature, spat in the general's food, or perhaps nothing at all. Working at the palace at the moment must be walking a tightrope for any but the most complacent, the most powerful. Governor Imnesh, an administrator sent from the capital, may be the sole person there who needs fear nothing.

Machine-maw clicks and blooms wide. It admits no light. However bright the day, from the outside its innards are always occluded, veiled in buffalo black. Each time she witnesses this, she braces for a jolt, a frisson of terror. Each time her nerves disappoint her with their strength, their indifference: no tear wells, no nausea clogs her throat. As though her time inside the kiln, those icy hours in her dying mother's arms, had been a dream. Vivid, but harmless.

The convicts are consigned one by one. There are greater kilns that can admit a dozen bodies at a time, and she hears of bigger ones still, the size of a factory. Entire landscapes devoted to converting the mortal coil into machine animus.

Nuawa does not linger, does not search the faces for any she might recognize or vice versa. She's built high, meticulous walls between her and sedition, refined her avoidance of dissidence into a scripture that she adheres to with the single-mindedness of a fanatic. Nothing to do with her. A stranger's misfortune.

Hands in the pockets of her coat, she moves on.

―――――――――

The tournament has been set up differently from the Marrow's seasons. Nuawa expected to be ushered into a crowded vestibule; instead there is an orderly line, each contestant taken aside one at a time. When her turn comes, the attendant puts a glass bead on her ear and a blindfold over her head. The fabric is light as chiffon but opaque as mortar, blotting out her vision entirely.

She is led through a corridor of kaleidoscope acoustics and obtuse light; the air anesthetizes, deadening her skin. Her head grows heavy. Each inhalation brings a rush of smoke, cloying and viscous.

When the blindfold falls away, she stirs to a golden warmth and a glassy day. Clear entirely, no clouds, the sky the color of poisonous frogs. Under her feet, sand moves like restless serpents, honeyed and hot. She breathes in salt. Heat pricks at her skin. A voice speaks in her ear. It is leeched of inflection, accent, even timbre; how a wooden puppet might sound like. "The labyrinth will test your strength, fortitude, and wit. To claim victory, find your way to its heart."

Nuawa turns around. The walls before her go on, carving up the sky, the scale and breadth of a giant's limbs. Made of pomegranate stone, gravid inside with thorn-knotted bones. Like a mass grave, a battlefield. And not real, that much her intellect can reason: The Marrow is large but not this large, the colors are too saturated to be nature. This is the world of her mother's painting. Her body must be shrouded in an enchantment of censors and intoxicants, prone and strapped down. It makes sense—with this, any sort of arena can be had, constructed to tournament specifications and mooting logistic issues. Phantasmagoria drugs are illicit, except evidently when used in a state capacity. It raises the question of whether injury sustained here will be real; whether damage here will manifest in physicality.

She touches the wall. Solid and lukewarm, a texture almost without friction. It gives and swings inward; once she is inside, it slides shut, seamless.

The harsh cries of birds fill her ears, a prayer tempo. Most likely, getting to the labyrinth's center is not the point—as ever, fighting is. Without a few shreds of flesh torn off, a few rivers-worth of gore, it would not be the Marrow. So she listens for human noises. Feet that must, of necessity, scuff against sand. A rustle of fabric, a murmur of voices. She takes off her boots—less sound to give her away. The rush of heat is euphoric, and for a moment she's half-tempted to sit and burrow into the sand; what could be the harm, after all.

Instead she draws her gun. Considers, briefly, the particulars of ammunition and firearms within this controlled hallucination. Whether they obey the same rules of wraith ricochet and ether gravity she knows, whether they produce recoil or require reloading.

What is certain is that the labyrinth does not adhere to architectural logic; even now the sky is already blotted out, the walls slanting inward and cutting the light to thin sheets. Each combatant would have entered through their own gate and there should be as many radiating pathways as there are competitors. Once there is only one duelist standing, the dream should end. No doubt she won't be the only one to have deduced this, and some of her competition would ally to secure triumph. Though even those would have to turn on each other in the end.

The path curves and slopes upward. Within the wall, some of the bones spasm into signs: a map, an arrow. Others flow and resolve into game-grids, in which chips of femur arrange themselves, twenty-three pieces to represent twenty-three duelists. Nuawa doesn't follow the arrow, quite, though it trails her with unnerving persistence. Herding her. Hardly any sport to be had if the course lasts too long and the combatants do not meet.

A thud of weapon on weapon. She stays behind, wishing that the walls were not so sheer and provided some footholds—the arena is created to force direct confrontations, all but prohibit ambush. When the noises quiet down, she rounds the corner and takes aim. Her shot connects.

Standing over the two bodies—one with a shadow shredded by her bullet, the other not—she appreciates that mirror guns appear to work here much as they do in the real world. Whichever oneirologist crafted this for the Marrow, they must be exceptional at detail. In the wall, the grid pulses and femur fragments unravel. Twenty-one.

By the time five pieces remain—not all of them Nuawa's doing—she has sustained a catalogue of injuries that attests to the diversity of techniques, styles, and weaponry: her mouth tastes of dead suns rising and ash spirals, hollowed-out anthills flicker in her vision, and a gash in her side is parched to a raw ache, as of jungle going to desert. Her shadow and spirit however she has guarded with resolve, accepted no more than a few shallow necessary cuts. Experience tells her those will be the most grievous wounds taken here, the most lasting in the physical world.

She hears the metallic scrape almost a heartbeat too late. As it is: sufficient time to dive out of the way when the knife hits, deflect it when the knife—torn out of soft sand, guided by its chain—darts by for a second strike. Her opponent is swaddled head to toe in strips of leather and wreaths of fabric, faceless, hanging slantwise to the wall. Feet like talons, digging into stone. An animal's grace. She thinks of the wolves around the village she grew up in, where Indrahi spirited her away until she was fifteen. Nuawa put down her share, mostly with bullet and once by blade, but even when she hunted them she found them magnetic. An existence of primal, easy purpose, nothing in them wasted or superfluous.

This faceless person is the only one she regrets defeating as her knife flowers in their stomach, a bloom of fractal slivers almost as bright as the eruption of viscera. To the end, they show no sign of fear or hesitation.

The game grid empties. One piece—Nuawa—remains.

When she wakes, it is to a room full of bodies lolling in chairs. Catatonic, head canted back or sideways, disarmed. Vulnerable. So is she: she reaches for, and finds herself without any of her weapons. A puncture on her arm, blood welling. She was the only one injected with the antidote to what must have been a fatal dose. The rest would be led to the ghost kiln, to be harvested unknowing. But then all sacrifices are sedated, and hearsay suggests there's a reason. As terror spoils meat in the slaughterhouse, perhaps serotonin sours the soul in the kiln-chamber, producing inferior ghosts.

Nuawa stands, blinking. A sick-sweet aroma lingers in the room. There is no window and the light is dim. She is, more or less, lucid. Her balance is good. Her head aches, the throb of a mild hangover. She wouldn't bet on herself in a fight right about now, but she's fit for self-defense. A glance: she looks for, and fails to find, the faceless duelist. Everyone lies with a face scarred or not, beautiful or ugly, but each is bare and plain to view. She counts, and recounts. Twenty-one faces, and her the twenty-second. And yet in the oneiric arena there were twenty-three.

A hand on her shoulder. She rounds, coiled for combat, to find a soldier. They stiffly present her a copper brooch the shape of a hyacinth, framed by tiny snowflakes. "Congratulations, duelist." When they look up she catches sight of their rank insignia; realizes they must be the new lieutenant, the one who received their commission in Jalsasskar. "General Lussadh has requested the pleasure of your company."

Entering the palace as a guest rather than supplicant is a peculiar experience, novel to Nuawa. Even entry is different, direct through the front gate, in carriage rather than on foot. The palace courtyard in the mirage-Sirapirat is crowded with topiary, kinnaree with enormous wings and elephants with killing tusks. The real one is smooth, just grass and trellises, the rare ever-green. The lieutenant leads her through the entrance hall, where portraits of the previous governors line either side, busts of winter's military heroes. Sirapirat's past rulers are absent,

Sirapirat gods barely allowed to be present. There are no shrines.

In the general's suite, she finds the parlor empty; is stiffly told by the lieutenant that the general—victor of a dozen wars, governor over ten provinces—will be present shortly.

This gives Nuawa time to appraise the chamber, though she supposes that this serves as merely a temporary office; the general's permanent residence is elsewhere, in the capital where the footpaths are made from elephant bones and buildings are carved of ice blocks, glazed and crowned in snow. Where white bears roam the streets, so they say, and the queen's handmaidens race each other in rooftop runs. Ice-girls, hair like sleet and eyes like tourmalines.

Almost nothing of the old palace has been retained save the wood floor. The curtains are new, monochrome pastels rather than the gold- and pearl-threaded textiles for which Sirapirat is known. Pale corals grown into divans, frosted glass tables, all acute angles and bold lines. White silk upholstery. A taxidermied hummingbird perches on one of the tables, looking as though it's about to take wing or burst into song. Beautiful, even exquisite, but foreign. Everything traces the queen's image, echoes her voice. Conjures her shadow, as though every piece of her possession must be stamped with her fingerprint.

Nuawa schools herself to show nothing.

Lussadh emerges from one of the inner doors, her hair damp. A cloud of fragrance—bath oils, soap—wreathes her, though her clothing is impeccable. It is less austere than what Nuawa last saw, but still pressed and crisp. The collars are open, baring clavicles. Hardly risqué, but Nuawa catches herself fascinated by the play of shadow at the base of the general's throat, the dip of bone there. The way Lussadh's skin runs bronzed-sienna under this light.

She forces her gaze away—aware that the general must notice—and tenses slightly. This is not like her. A remnant of the dream drug has loosened her thoughts, dampening her reason.

"I owe you a second apology," Lussadh says. "For what I did back in that library. I do have my reasons, but it must have seemed irregular and I understand Sirapirat has strict ideas regarding chastity."

Only for nobility, of an era past, and families with ties to high administration. Or if she were a monk. But she says simply, "Not at my age, General. I'm long past maiden-time and have never sought ordainment. In any case, what you did would impair no one's chastity, even in the strictest of Sirapirat households."

"How does one ... impair the Sirapirat concept of chastity?"

"The same one would any other, I should think. Provided the subject is chaste to start with." Nuawa folds her hands before her. She has studied the literature that Lussadh likes, acidic poetry and pragmatic strategy, tragedies of families rent and radical philosophy. Nuawa is nothing if not a quick study, a chameleon of thought-schools. Last time she was not prepared— this time, she is. "As for Sirapirat's national chastity, that was forfeited centuries past. We have been occupied before, as most countries have been. Doubtless far back in our ancestry, primitive tribal hunters vied for supremacy or grazing rights."

It works as she meant it to: the general looks at her and laughs unbridled and sudden. Pleased without being flattered, acknowledging the slight jab that nevertheless admits Sirapirat is not new to conquest—that the Winter Queen is not especially brutal, especially immoral, is merely acting out the natural consequence of human expansion. And therefore Her Majesty cannot be held any more or less accountable than bygone conquerors or those apocryphal tribes. "You are made to cut, aren't you? So sharp. Please, have some of this."

Food is served, a basket of flatbreads and bowls of chutney, a yellow curry. Both sight and smell seize Nuawa, oneiric after-effect amplifying her appetite. It demands; she accedes—her eating is ravenous, neat; with its ubiquity she has become adept at having Kemiraj cuisine without smearing and spilling everywhere. It is good, warming, the exact kind of fare that chases out the chill. Such fare has become popular for more reason than just the general's favor.

"Fighting's hungry work," the general says. "So much I can attest."

Common ground extended, as though negotiating a treaty. She is regarded if not as equal in status, then at least a type of professional colleague. Nuawa wipes her hands on a warm, wet cloth. "We think ourselves as creatures of intellect, mind over matter, soul ascendant over flesh. But the stomach growls and we eat. The skin commands and we obey. Nerves respond to stimuli and we are helpless to the fact. It's almost, I think, shameful."

Lussadh cleans her plate, meticulous. Wasting nothing. "I watched you fight."

Duelist pride pushes her to fish for compliments. Prudence pushes her to say, "It's my sincere wish that I could provide the general with suitable diversion, however fleeting."

A guttering *hah*. "Giving praise for your techniques seems superfluous. You're consummate at killing and you know it well. Those dream drugs though, they are tremendous. Any battlefield can be conjured, from sheer fancy and cruelty alike, from history or fable. Called *maya* in Sirapirat's precursor language, aren't they, such vivid hallucinations?"

"Loanword from the ecclesiastic register, General."

"Not a distinction of which most Sirapirat natives are aware." A smile pricks the corners of Lussadh's mouth. "Might I offer you accommodation at the palace? It's close to the Marrow and ought to be more convenient for you."

Her stomach twitches. Crawls, slightly, with suspicion. "I am honored," Nuawa says. "But I'm not sure I warrant such treatment. It seems an unusual privilege to extend."

"So it is, but my aide is an admirer of yours. He was most

insistent that I treat you well and would be very cross if I didn't try."

No doubt, if the aide in question even exists. Lussadh wants to monitor her closely. The why will have to wait for later: it could be anything, from her background to the circumstances of their first meeting. "This is overwhelming generosity." And an opportunity, cutting both ways, to get close to the general. "I will not slight you by rejecting it."

SIX

NUAWA SENDS WORD, BY COURIERS OF FEATHERED SHADOW and fissured dream, to her mother. The message would arrive piecemeal and circumspect, a fruit-laden twig on the table, a red cicada on the window, mercury beads where no liquid has been spilled. Indrahi is no stranger to slotting code and cant together, produce from them useful meaning — she was the one who taught Nuawa after all, and back in the days being the master of seditious intelligence let her elude capture whole and well-off. Nuawa always wanted to ask her mother how it was that she could not save Tafari, but that question is beyond even Nuawa's power of candor. More amputation than reopening a wound.

On their part, Tezem is beyond elated, cocksure that Lussadh's invitation to the palace is a sign of the highest favor. That even if Nuawa's first victory is her last, Tezem's fortune is all but made for the next several years. Nuawa doesn't see the connection, but they aren't the only one to indulge in this fantasy. As the news of her living arrangement spreads — the velocity of wildfire — four of Sirapirat's best managers contacted her with offers of patronage. She's turned them all down, more for convenience than out of allegiance to Tezem. Now is not the time for negotiating new contracts.

She takes stock of her new accommodation. Twice the size of her apartment in Matiya, ten times as ostentatious and no less outlandish than Lussadh's suite. The same pastel upholstery and curtains, furniture in azure glass and cinderous resin rather than coral. Unthinkable opulence, even the ghosts given a diet so fine that they are almost inaudible, invisible, perhaps even happy. Tributes to the queen and taxes fund this, and the newer a constituent, the higher the tax rates.

A hallway separates her from the general. She is surprised Lussadh hasn't outright sent an attendant to shadow her, though no doubt some form of surveillance is present within the suite. A toilet is attached to her room, but for ablutions she is to share the wing's bath-chamber with Lussadh.

In spite of everything, she is elated; accomplished, even. This close to the general. The rest, she thinks as she fingers the drapes around her new bed, is a clear and straight line. It will require wit, effort, unstinting vigilance. But it is plausible.

She has a couple days before the next match, and while she's sustained no injury she doesn't want to risk an ether infection. The general has offered her the palace chiurgeon, but she demurred saying that she prefers her own. Not untrue. The palace chiurgeon, like most high-ranking officials, is from the capital and loyal first to the governor and the general. Few native Sirapirat serve at the palace above the rank, at best, of clerks.

It takes some circumnavigation to reach her chiurgeon's clinic, an informal practice above a bookshop. Past teak shelves and stacks of secondhand volumes, she climbs the scuffed steps to a door. Knocks. It cracks open grudgingly.

Rakruthai is one of those people who will always look ageless, though of late the seams and crosshatched nooks are beginning to show. Mid-forty and male today, to go by the upturned collars. The chiurgeon doesn't always signal it so clearly, but most of the time also doesn't much care whether they're assumed to be woman, man, or neither. It is immaterial to his profession and his patients accord him reverence however he dresses or speaks. He gives Nuawa a glance, up and down. No greetings.

She makes a half-curtsy. "I need a consultation."

He tuts. "I've got a chronic fatigue sufferer in fifteen, twenty minutes."

The clinic is lit by silvery daylight coming in through the wide windowpane. Expensive scrolls on the wall. They stir gently, moved by a breeze of their own, echoing air currents in a land far off. Where Rakruthai hails from, perhaps, though he has adopted a Sirapirat name. It is forever bandied about that he was a chiurgeon to some head of state, then winter happened as it so often does, and Rakruthai's position became untenable. Nuawa does not know the specifics and does not press, though like anyone else she is curious.

The chiurgeon pushes a chair toward her. "Your shadow looks in good shape. You don't look dead on your feet. No crippling injuries. What do you want?"

"I'd like to protect myself from poisoning, curses, and grudges. A little like what Yifen's got."

Rakruthai peers at her over the rim of his spectacles. "Really. Her modification was begun when she was a child, carved onto her one piece at a time, and she's an expert practitioner. It isn't a shortcut to immunity against all harm and ills; it is a lifetime of *discipline* and devotion."

"Some lesser form must exist," Nuawa says. "I need it for just a month, two at most."

"Some lesser form must exist," he mimics in falsetto. "It doesn't. Not safely."

"If it's less dangerous than being poisoned by the competition, doctor, I'll consider the risk more than worthwhile." Or cursed by someone in the palace, someone in the army, who would see her as a rival in Lussadh's favor. There are infinite permutations of potential enemies; she intends to avoid most of them.

Rakruthai snorts. "Very well. I'll have something prepared for you, but note that it will cost you dearly. Speaking of which, you've been drawing a lot of attention. I don't mean from your field." He pulls an envelope from under a paperweight. "Someone knows I'm your physician and left this at my window. I opened it. Sorry."

He doesn't seem particularly sorry, though Nuawa would grant that he has good reason to check the contents. The envelope is thin leather, the paper inside browned and ink-spotted. Its author has an unsteady hand, but her name is spelled out clearly: *For Nuawa Dasaret.* The blots and crossed-out sections tell her they are used to a horizontal script rather than a vertical one. Not a native speaker of Ughali, then. The message begins with a line from Vahatma's second banner of radiance: *That which bends does not always break.* The following verses are a selection of scripture ruminating on the cycle of rebirth and reincarnation.

"So?" Rakruthai leans forward.

"Bad theology. Bad allegory." She rereads the ending stanza, which is not from any scripture she knows of: *Under deeds of righteous vengeance, from a river of blood and sand, Vahatma may once more rise.* Textually it makes no sense; Vahatma—in scripture—has never fallen, endures as eternally as the wheel of consequence. The only Vahatma that has ever been vanquished is the one that stood in defense of Sirapirat. "Really clumsy. Maybe I have a particularly shy fan." She puts the envelope away in her jacket. "It's nothing."

Her second stop takes her away from the genteel streets around Rakruthai's clinic, away from the low, curling gardens that garland the respectable households in ice-bitten evergreens. It is not that the Filament House is disreputable; it is more that its clientele and commodities are foreign, and a quality that carries with it a specific stigma. But this once, foreign is exactly what Nuawa wants.

The Filament House is secluded behind a thicket of tall tenements, away from the immediate business of the boulevard. Even its architecture does not belong, tessellated arcades and balconies, a façade of bricks and painted stone. Oblong windows done in jagged tracery and tinted panes. She is admitted into a partitioned lounge—discretion so highly prized here that customers need never see one another—and asked whether she has an appointment. "No," she says, "but I'd like to make one. I have a reference from Yifen Lin." She tells the attendant her preferences. Specific, even outlandish, though she knows it is not unique to her.

"That member of our staff is ready and can see you at once," the attendant says, "if you wish."

Nothing like immediate gratification. "Do I get a quote now, or later?"

She gets one. The price is high, but then the Filament provides services like nowhere else. For certain niches, it has no competitor. Once payment has been negotiated, she is led past softly lit corridors. From all accounts, the Filament is selective in the patrons it accepts; at any time there might be only a dozen guests in the house or fewer. Privacy is paramount and, despite the upfront talk of commerce, there is an illusion that this is a personal rather than a transactional arrangement.

The room is faultlessly clean. Furniture in cerise and lavender, the ghost-pipes a quiet murmur, decorated so it would offend no one and fade into the background. If adjacent rooms are in use, she hears no noise. Soundproofing must have gobbled up much of the establishment's initial funding. A plate of marzipan fruits has been provided for her, miniature rose apples and pears glazed to a high, succulent shine. She tries one. It is rich, soft, lightly sweet rather than saccharine. Pleasant, surprisingly so.

Nuawa doesn't have to wait long. Part of the service is the impression of effortlessness, everything moving along with the ease of dream logic. Perfect, exquisite.

The courtesan glides into the room, a rustle of leather and polished boots. She has a sculpted face, acute chin and narrow jaw, an umber complexion. The look of a Kemiraj aristocrat, but it is the manner more than the appearance that compels. She takes Nuawa's chin in her hand, tilting it up. "And how should I take you?" A low thrumming voice, tenor.

"You are presuming."

"Am I wrong?"

Nuawa does not pull free. In bed, most partners assume she'd take charge and she does; it is rare that yielding excites her, rarer still that she finds a bedmate who suits her in that way. "I'm not the first to come here for this." A semi-popular fantasy, or at least one where clients are few but which pays exceptionally well.

The courtesan laughs; she is no Lussadh but must have studied the general well, mimicking even the edged amusement, the exact timbre. "No, but you are the first to talk so much. Come, it is a play and this room is our stage. Fall into it. You wished for a certain thing, but is it not the unpredictable parts that excite?"

There is persuasive force behind this person, an intensity of play-acting that convinces. Nuawa gives; the courtesan guides her to the wall, pressing her against the padded hardwood. It should feel methodical, flimsy make-believe, but her mood and circumstances conspire. When the courtesan undoes her trousers —none too gently—and slips a gloved finger inside, she is already slick, nerve-ends eager for touch. She breathes deeply to pace herself, delay the cresting of arousal, as two long fingers become three. Embroidered suede. Attention has been paid to detail, to texture. The push and the pull, a curl of knuckle that insistently grazes those nerve-ends, a thumb and forefinger that press and pinch. This side of agony.

She is maneuvered: her arms pinned behind her—she could easily break free; she doesn't—and her head canted back against the cool silk of the wall. Hard teeth work at her throat while one gloved hand pulls her up, up until she is on tiptoes. Straining to stay upright, the muscles of her calves trembling as those long fingers move inside her.

By the time she's flung onto the bed and spread, her breathing has gone to rags and her pulse raw. Lussadh (*not quite, but enough*) says, "Ask for it."

"Yes—" Predictable, even this part, but in momentum the body overwhelms the intellect: Nuawa does not care that this is pretense, that the script itself follows a type.

"Ask again. This time properly."

"Please." She closes her eyes; she imagines. "General."

Coming down from climax, she lies splayed on the sheets, her cunt fluttering. She is stripped from the waist down while the courtesan never disrobed at all. The gloves will be scrupulously washed, Nuawa supposes, but the Filament's laundry deals with more sordid secretions daily. "You seem to enjoy your work," she says. "The mechanics if not the client."

The courtesan leans next to the door, hands loose at her sides. "And this seems very good for you, medicinal even. *She* inspires frustration, doesn't she? A most magnetic personage."

Nuawa wonders if she should feel embarrassment, but it is no different than treating a fever, dressing a wound. Her thighs are damp, her limbs leaden with euphoria. Satisfying the flesh is easy, and this way is safer than most. "Anywhere I can clean up?"

"I could clean you. It'd be no chore."

A tone of intimacy that is good at sounding genuine rather than the ingratiation of worker to client. "No, I'm fine."

"As you wish. I'll send for someone to bring warm water, towels." The courtesan nods. "Good luck in the games, duelist. Come again should you feel the need."

SEVEN

LUSSADH IS GOING THROUGH THE OUTPUT OF SIRAPIRAT'S agriculture with Governor Imnesh when the reports come in.

"Taxing them at this rate isn't sustainable," she is telling Imnesh. "The farmsteads here have mostly adapted, but even you must admit that the landowners and farmers don't have enough left to seed the next harvest."

"They're still sheltering dissidents, General." Imnesh has his hands folded on the table, though she suspects he yearns to clench them into fists, then apply those fists to her face. An older courtier — senior to her in age if not in rank — he's never been one to curry favor with Lussadh, mostly because he was close to her predecessor and after all this time still resents what he sees as usurpation. "Five decades on and they haven't learned their place. No one wants my position."

She gazes at the cabinet behind him, a display of medals and badges earned in combat. Ex-soldiers from before her time tend to hold the same opinion of her: an upstart who stole the position of winter's commander, second only to the queen's rank as grand marshal. A position that should have gone to one of the old guard. "I just put down an uprising in Kavaphat, Imnesh. I know what it means when seditionists operate as guerillas. But brutalizing their supporters only inspires the next batch and when all the farmers are dead, they won't be able to pay a lick of tax." She doesn't say that she did not approve of his most recent mass execution. There are limits to how far she can push. "We've been treating Sirapirat citizens like animals for fifty years. Past the first decade or so it got excessive, and the result is we *still* have problems. Consider Kemiraj." Of which she is the de facto governor.

"Yes, yes. Kemiraj joined winter as a *very* special case. You of all people know, General, and can afford to gently handle it. Leniency is no panacea. Indeed I have been milder and milder with this city, treating it like my own infant, and what do I get."

Caricatures of him published in satirical boards. Petty and harmless, an insult Imnesh could easily have let slide. Lussadh suspects he doesn't even get dead animals in his bed and, against all odds, hasn't yet been successfully poisoned. "There is such a thing as responding in proportion. Give them a couple years. Send as many to the kilns as is absolutely necessary and not one person more. Have them give tribute at the same rate as Johramu."

"That's half the current tribute, General."

"I'm aware."

"Where," he says, enunciating deliberately as though speaking to a child, "am I supposed to find the ghosts to compensate for that shortfall?"

"Kavaphat, for the next six months. It won't be your problem." Not that the capital requires such surplus. There are entire vaults of ghosts frozen and dreaming their unknowable, foggy fantasies. "After that, we'll see. Get to it swiftly, Imnesh, and incidentally reconsider your choice of having Sirapirat staff *only* for menial positions—you do realize having them in the kitchen and garden is a fine way to have your food spat in or poisoned. Either have locals in supervising roles as well, or you'll have to allocate a higher stipend to hire menials from the capital. We'll talk again tomorrow."

In her study she draws out her calling-glass, slots it into a mount. The palace staff has filled her quarters with flowers, vases bristling with lilac bloom and bifurcated leaves. Potted ferns that look like they have teeth, either to appease her taste — what they think is her taste — or to make a statement against a symbol of winter's rule. No further dead birds. "Report," she says.

A hazy image from the calling-glass: the body of one of her soldiers. Ulamat holds up resin sheets of more images, three more bodies. Each has been decapitated, the head cradled in the body's lap or perched on the body's shoulder. "As you can see, my lord."

She eyes the fragment of Ytoba's phalange on her desk, a yellowed piece nestling in sable fabric. In her personal vault, she has an extensive collection of such, a piece or two of every dangerous enemy: a lock of hair, a shard of bone. Grudge detritus, necessary for a thaumaturge to track a person down. Which the palace thaumaturge had, or so she'd thought. When the result pointed to four different locations in the city, she'd sent a soldier to each for reconnaissance. "I can see. My thanks, Ulamat."

"I would never overstep my bounds, lord, but this seems like a case I ought to know about."

"It is," she says. "In due time. What about the duelist?"

He leaves the body, letting a Sirapirat officer have a turn at examining it. "I've been looking into her family. A distressingly common surname, mostly attached to people who aren't related. Not native to Sirapirat, as such; the surname belongs to a wave of immigrants who arrived here during the administration of—"

"Ulamat," Lussadh says mildly.

"Yes, my lord, apologies. I wasn't able to find immediate relation save a cousin who entered monkhood—teaches at a theological college in Kavaphat—and an aunt living in the countryside; nothing troubling so far. The aunt used to live in Johramu, came back twenty-five years ago presumably to raise the duelist, who was orphaned. Was born illegitimate, I get the impression. The aunt, Indrahi Dasaret, sent her to exceptionally fine schools until she was seventeen."

"No university?" An odd choice, surely, since Sirapirat boasts a decent one and Nuawa strikes Lussadh as well-educated.

His breath curls out. He is standing alone on a balcony, gaining distance from the scene and the corpse. "Not as far as I've been able to find out. Private tutoring, I reckon. The aunt appears moderately well-off. I'm tracing the source of her wealth, just in case."

"I appreciate it." She pauses. "You are not going to look into why my soldiers died. Not until I tell you. It is important, but I have my reasons, for now."

"Here as in all else I bow to your decision. One tangential matter. There is a Kemiraj courtesan at the Filament House in Sirapirat, who—ah—tenders unique services. That is, she is a sort of thespian, dressing as you do and ..."

"That I didn't need to know, Ulamat."

"No, no. I keep an eye on the courtesan because her clientele, while a short list, is of some interest. But naturally not an item I would bring to your attention unless it's relevant. Most recently, the duelist joined the exclusive list of those giving her patronage."

Lussadh blinks. The muscles in her face spasm between pulling into a grimace and something else. "Are you absolutely certain your informant didn't confuse a stranger for Nuawa."

"My *lord*." Indignation. "I wasn't there to monitor her myself, but they are very sure, absolutely."

"Of course."

She makes herself tea, strong, the color of desert dusk. Pours generously, and starts sipping while it can scald. It is not that the idea surprises; she is a public figure, and even if she had not conquered territories in her queen's name her position would nevertheless inspire deep loathing, resentment, fury. That some of it would translate to *that* is not new—she has seen porno-graphic art featuring her, ranging from risqué to profane, and heard of worse. There is the other kind: she is not unaware of her own appeal, has never been since her days as royalty. But perhaps she has been too forward with the duelist, has taken liberties which Nuawa cannot safely refuse and so must find an outlet for.

Teacup in hand, Lussadh paces the parlor she shares with Nuawa then—after some consideration—unlocks the duelist's room. She already knows from the servants that Nuawa has brought very little. The wardrobe contents are sparse, practical, with a few formal outfits: a narrow dress, a limned jacket, close-cut trousers with snaking lines of seed pearls. No jewelry save the victor's badge from the first round. Toiletries are likewise few and simple, with a particular preference for herbs in toothpaste, soap. No perfume or cosmetics. No telling details, like keepsakes or religious icons. Nor signs that the duelist practices alchemy of the spirit, or indeed any other sort. That the duelist is literate is obvious, but she appears to have left all her reading behind.

In all, her belongings have been curated to reveal next to nothing: not her faith or pastimes, and certainly not her politics. Reasonably cautious rather than something to hide, perhaps.

Lussadh reviews the other contestants. She's met most of them, felt no pull of affinity, though she won't discount them yet. There is a handful she wants to verify for good measure. But it's rare for a tribute game to yield a glass-bearer, let alone several. These are spectacles for the public more than for the queen, who takes no interest. But given that Lussadh has found a potential bearer, it's odd that Her Majesty hasn't come to Sirapirat herself —normally shows little patience when it comes to the matter of her mirror's pieces.

She spends the afternoon with the games. Initially she was concerned that she would have to share the hallucination, but the oneirologist behind it is ingenuous. The arenas, transmitted through specially treated beads, doesn't require that Lussadh imbibe the drugs. The pane she uses is concave and immense, panoramic. An eagle's eye view of the whole, then a focus on each combatant as she needs. It is orderly and she wishes the same could be had in the physical world, the vantage point of a god over battlefields. The way the queen saw the world before her mirror broke, so she says. She has never shared how it shattered, or why, or what she intends once she has found the last glass-bearer. *I have been looking a long time,* she would say, and there she would stop.

There are two bouts scheduled today. Two more tomorrow. Expedient, all told, four hundred whittled down to one dozen in no time.

The first arena is an occidental temple, long corridors like fingers and stained-glass images of the afterlife in fire and flagellation. Candelabras make shadows of duelists as they meet and fight in tabernacles, triumph in chapels, fall on altars. Like a studied painting, this arena too is made in detail, with an architect's eye. It is tremendous work, like all the previous arenas, as much imagination as realism. She must meet the oneirologist, Lussadh decides. Perhaps she could commission them for the next tournament.

The next is an underground cavern built like a honeycomb. Quartz deposits pock its walls, small rutilated knuckles buried in blunt rock. The duelists are separated by chambers where water congeals drool-thick and ink-dark, and razorish forms scurry by in flocks. A backdrop less inspired than the rest, though Lussadh supposes from each duelist's perspective it is more dimensional. More menacing. As battlefields go, the challenges lie in visibility, maneuverability.

Her attention pulls inevitably to Nuawa. The duelist is a

silhouette, sharp animation obverse to the dark, running down a lopsided passage. She fights with a soldier's economy, not a duelist's sensibility for spectacle and grandeur. Lussadh thinks back to the university library, to the completed bounty she hears of afterward. When most duelists wage battle with exhibitionist flourish, Nuawa's efficiency stands out.

It is not fast, and it is not neat, but out of twenty-five Nuawa is the last one standing.

———

Rakruthai pronounces her hale, *in mercantile condition*, a turn of phrase Nuawa has always found endearingly cynical. "Though not if you keep taking oneiric drugs." He peels off his gloves, drops them into a septic jar, where they float deflated and bereft in the blue fluid: dead skin. "You're verging on dependency. The doses you had were brutal and, long-term, they'll fuck you up well and proper. I'll give you something to ease it. Side effect is mild anemic symptoms for a couple weeks, three."

"Will I be fit for combat?" Nuawa is on her stomach, the wood-and-stone slab hard under her, separated from her skin by a thin sheet.

"Sure. Someone would have to break most of your limbs to keep you out of the arena." He frowns. "I'm not your mother."

"For both our sakes, I would hope not."

"What *does* your family think? I know you have some. Even you couldn't spring fully formed from the ether."

She puts her head back down, imagines herself that way, a creature of untouchable fortitude sloughing off ice: her bones would be iron, her skin hermetic as carapace. The idea cannot help but entice. To be something that self-contained, literally self-made. "Maybe I did." Instead she was drawn out of a ghost kiln, should have been a corpse. Her memory does not predate being six, though she supposes the same is true for most. Preverbal, toddler years aren't the most memorable. "Or maybe I'm an orphan and you're being insensitive."

The chiurgeon makes a small needling noise as he puts on fresh gloves. "What of that? You don't have feelings. Here we are." The hiss of depressurized air. "Keep still; don't be alarmed. It'll hurt. This needs to enter your veins, live in your body. I thought of making an incision and inserting it as a charm, but you'll complain that you can't fight then."

Nuawa doesn't feel anything, a bite, a pinch at the base of her spine. Then the legs, wriggling as they burrow into subcutaneous fat, striking nerves and veins the way machines strike gold, strike arteries of precious gems. Legs and antennae like surgical razors. It feels enormous, though it can't be; her sense of scale dilates.

"What *was* that?" she asks as Rakruthai disinfects her back. The alcohol stings, but much less than the pain of insertion.

"A parasite," the chiurgeon says, matter of fact. "Half-real in this stage of growth; you can't see it with the naked eye and you shouldn't feel it move too much. It gobbles up curses and toxins like nothing else. Food too, so you'll have to get bigger helpings than usual. Don't recommend keeping it for longer than ten months—it'll have matured by then and will be trying to use you as a nest. Reproduces asexually. Little ones, you see, not a litter but an entire swarm."

"What do they look—" Nuawa bites down on her lip. "Never mind. Can I get up?"

"Yes. Take these after you've had your last compulsory arena dose; it'll replicate the oneiric drugs, but more gently so you don't go into withdrawal. Twice a day for the first couple weeks, then once a day until it's finished."

"Thank you, doctor." The tablets Rakruthai give her rattle in their jar, tiny discs dyed scarab-green.

"There's a second letter for you." He tosses her an envelope. "I'm getting sick of being your unpaid courier. What *is* this about exactly? I couldn't open the damn thing."

Grimacing, Nuawa tears the message out. It must have been witched to unseal only at her touch. The same handwriting, the same pattern of mistakes, though the ink blots are fewer this time. Vahatma again, then segueing into proverbs. The second page is not text at all but diagrams, detailed and drawn with an engineer's precision. And though she is not one, she recognizes this for what it is. The inner workings and anatomy of the god-engine Vahatma. Copied down from some lost, banned volume.

"Something dangerous," she says. "*Do* you want to see it?"

Perhaps it is her tone, or perhaps Rakruthai is that risk-averse, but the chiurgeon waves her aside. "No thanks. Can you tell whoever this is to leave me out of it?"

"I'll try."

Nuawa dresses slowly, tender from the operation, and wraps herself in insulating layers. Chamois leather coat, a gift from Tezem. She's never seen the animal from which it is derived, native to provinces that have always been cold and did not change much with winter. Around Sirapirat, most wildlife and cattle guttered out in a matter of decades. Vast fields punctuated by animal dead, preserved until they were stripped and put to purpose: hide, horns, hooves. What it must be like to be a creature of the wild when the queen first came, every ancestral instinct gone to brittle chaff, every channel of information wrenched perpendicular to its original self.

Occasionally she wonders what rice grown in paddies rather than in glasshouses tastes like, smells like, harvests so plentiful that even the poorest could eat bowl after bowl. She should ask her mother when they can speak again safely. Indrahi would be following the tournament. *What does your family think?* Proud, Nuawa could have said. She is not her brother, who is so removed from her and her mother, has been since twelve—the youngest a temple would ordain a novice—that he is a stranger. Their faces have never resembled one another's, their inclinations even less. It is not that she resents his cowardice any more than a hawk resents a mouse, more that she disdains his dishonesty, his piety as an excuse.

The month is unseasonable, escalating to frigid much sooner than usual. Seasons run according to the queen's temperament and proximity: by all accounts the capital is nearly uninhabitable, an ecosystem built on hostility against human life, not that it keeps her court empty. Quite the opposite, despite the shortage of heating. Everyone wants to be close to the throne.

She veers toward the nearby market, hands cupped over her mouth for heat. In her haste to minimize her belongings in the palace, she'd forgotten some conveniences. Favorite soaps, fruit candies. There's a confectioner who stocks crystallized mangoes and jackfruits, expensive treats Indrahi would spoil her with when she was little. Perhaps she'll buy a gift for Rakruthai. It pays to treat one's doctor well.

The confectioner's is crowded, gold-drops and gold-cups in boxes, painted wooden cases full of chocolates dusted with tea powder, sugar sculptures everywhere. Loud children and fretting guardians. She picks a generous basket of crystallized fruits, pineapple, jackfruit, tamarinds. Pricey; worthwhile. On the way out, she catches sight of a pet stall. The chiurgeon often complains that he can't afford to replace his snake, dead of an infection several months past. She'll bill it to Tezem.

Musky odors waft from the cages and the pens, barnyard smells, damp fur and feed. They are ventilated and diffused by the cold air, though at close quarters they are inescapable, unself-conscious. It isn't pleasant but she likes the novelty, standing among so much animal mass, their cacophonic warmth. Owls tethered to their perches, a couple of svelte blue-back goats, an albino python in a terrarium. The goats have gorgeous eyes, side-ways pupils as alien as they are mesmeric.

"Want to touch them? The goats are of the finest pedigree. Superstitious occidents stay away from them though, but what can you do. Supposedly their demons look like goats."

Nuawa starts, caught off-guard, mortified to have given childlike admiration to a common animal. "Ziya. This is a dramatic career change."

"Diversifying business interests, my girl." He rubs the side of his face. "Animals are kinder to deal with than most people."

She doesn't disagree. "I'm interested in the python. Wait, is *that* for sale?"

Ziya gives a show of his teeth, one incisor missing, from a brawl or age she has never been able to tell. "This lives with me, so no. Beautiful, isn't it?"

The husky enchants even more than the goats, tall and thickly built, draped in an ombré coat. Deep sienna gradating to a belly like pale fire, the eyes like a clear sky. On an occidental, such irises look peculiar and wrong; on this animal they look right, pretty. She kneels and strokes the dog's ochre head, the cartilage-in-velvet ears. It regards her, tail twitching, and despite herself she grins. Its body radiates furnace heat.

"Take it for a walk," Ziya says. "Give it fifteen, twenty minutes. Real exercise if you reach Wat Totsanee. It's been getting restless and fat, and I haven't the time. We'll talk about your snake when you're back."

A gift; she doesn't argue. Nor does she need a leash. At Ziya's direction, the husky follows, trotting level with her.

In the crowd it navigates, meeting no resistance, picking a direction through and out of the market. Comprehending Sirapirat's topography more thoroughly than any human native: wolf intellect parlayed, adapted to streets and architecture. Made for one purpose, better suited to the cold than most. Easy to like this creature as it moves alongside her, much easier than any person or child.

Wat Totsanee is quiet this time of the day, the yard scant save for novices shoveling snow, sweeping evergreen detritus. It's not one of the temples she frequents, its walls enclosing no more than one scriptorium and a prayer hall. Smattering of shrines to large-bellied Totsanee, snake-armed Sravasti, minor icons with the faces of elephants or eagles. Of city temples, this is one of the most minor; Nuawa leaves offerings in the form of currency. Now that her rent for the Matiya apartment is suspended, she has coin to spare. The novices recognize Ziya's hound. One bhikkuni waves to the dog, brandishing a varnished tibia. This must be some agreed-upon, familiar game; it leaps at once into the chase.

The husky in motion is a marvel, bulky muscles working beneath umber-and-white, legs built for running put to their paramount directive. The bhikkuni, despite her fleece and billowing robes, keeps ahead for several solid minutes before the hound catches her. Even then she puts up a good fight, wrestling the hound away, keeping the bone out of its reach. Nuawa is vestigial to the event, but she is content to watch from under the canopy of Sravasti's serpent-limbs.

"Wild things are so magnificent until they are tamed. It robs them, taming, of their vital beauty. What's left behind is soft as loam beneath sleet, as forgettable. One domesticated thing is much like another. Furniture. Appliances. Ghosts."

The cold first, before the sight. Senses rouse to urgent stimuli far in advance of cognition, the vanguard: the heart clogging, the blood in roar, the muscles locking into paralysis. Nuawa fights against it as she turns. The Winter Queen, then. Behind the shrine, just out of sight of the novices or the bhikkuni busy with the hound. A hundred sets of calculation fleet through Nuawa, a hundred sets of admonitions and cautions from her mother. They collide with a single image, of the queen in martial regalia, the formal wear of mass executions.

"Your Majesty," Nuawa says, poised to perform obeisance; bending the knee is a price so miniscule it is not one at all. She does not think of the envelope stashed away in her shirt.

"As you were." The queen is in softer garb than in Nuawa's memory, sleeveless fitted bodice and damask robe. Uncovered shoulders, one breast bare. Her flesh is oddly hairless, nearly without pores, the impossible smoothness of steel. Eyes like onyx, black on black on black. "You are the one my general has taken in."

"Yes, Majesty." Speed of draw, Nuawa thinks, and the queen alone. Now that the animal part of her has relaxed its hold, flight instinct gone, it is time to evaluate alternatives. What were the stories of assassins, the attempts? Did she not study them the way a student chiurgeon studies mortality's anatomy? Much of her mind is wasteland, but it is reconstituting. "I serve her, and as she lives in your name so I must live in yours." It is empty flattery, stalling for time.

The queen's smile does not show teeth, an expression like the profile of a knife. "Do you? But you have the mien of a wild thing, not tamed at all, not yet."

All assassins have failed. Nuawa has pored over each case, as much information as she could get, as much as Indrahi could obtain. Some of it was inevitable propaganda, shoring up the queen's myth and might, an avatar of season and storm — elemental force, unstoppable. Lethal at a touch, a glance. But no matter the embellishments, the queen has survived assassins for longer (four times as, six times as; the number is not easy to pin down, nor is it relevant) than Nuawa has been alive. "I am what I am, Your Majesty," is all she says.

The royal mouth widens; the monarchic features soften. Tenderness, sudden and inexplicable. "Put your hands here, both of them."

Where the queen can see them, Nuawa supposes. She flattens her palms on the shrine, at Sravasti's feet, fingers splayed out. The wood is rime-dusted, though she can't feel it much — good gloves. The queen leans forward, exhales. Almost at once the wood goes white, Sravasti blanching from brass to glacier.

Time dilates. Frostbite seems a small, inadequate word; Nuawa's world narrows down to this one point of contact, to the nerves in her hands and the epidermis that serves as their flimsy armor. The body overloads, is confounded, cold translating to high burn as if her ligaments have become coal, blistered and cinderous. The wood creaks, then cracks. She is beyond sensation.

"Lift your arms." Winter's voice, hypnotic.

Nuawa does so. The ice shivers and gives; her hands are free. She flexes them, moving her fingers. They are mobile and, when she shakes her gloves off, she discovers her hands intact. Anticipation and knowledge posit grotesque knuckles, blasted nails, late-stage frostbite. But all that has happened is that her hands are red. A piece of the shrine hisses and falls, splinters and icicles. A build-up of frost has covered the ground. Rime has gathered on her coat, in her scarf, on her eyelashes. The world is scintillant.

"Yes," croons the queen. "This is so fine, so excellent, how strong. I should take you to a place where you may wake and grow, full of puzzles for you to solve. I should take you home, where you can run very fast—see, like that dog you so admire."

Something under the shrine, a piece of support perhaps, snaps and collapses. "I believe the general was waiting to introduce me to you formally, Your Majesty." Her hands sting and throb but they are whole, nearly undamaged. Everything works, joints capable, fingertips alert. Nor have her lips fused shut, one more miracle to accompany the rest.

"She'd want formality, ceremony; that is in her breeding. And —" The queen stops. "Lussadh is a creature of supreme intuition, until she is not."

She is gone without drawing the novices' attention, exit as abrupt as entrance. Omnipresent, not only in her element but in the world she has created: all of winter her domain, in every sense.

Nuawa collects the husky. She does not stay to explain the property damage.

EIGHT

Nuawa emerges from her third—and last—oneiric match. Her muscles feel heavy, sore, as though she'd exerted herself physically. She blinks up at the gray ceiling and draws in a sip of the murky, cloying air. She tries to remember the fight and discovers that she has only the faintest recollection. All around her, the other duelists sleep on; one or two have slid down to the floor, splayed and slack as any corpse, breathing shallowly. Her head aches, the tang of drug in her mouth like copper and unripe fruit. The site of injection in her arm has swelled, bruising darkly.

She pushes herself to her feet and staggers. Her knees are as weak as the rest of her. The dose was much stronger than usual, double or triple the strength. She presses the heel of her palm to her brow, finds it damp with sweat. Several attempts later and she is upright, laboring step by step toward the door. Tezem's personnel are there to greet and congratulate her; she stares at them a moment before waving them off. Everything around her is either moving too fast or too slow. Her blood beats hot and thunderous behind her breastbone.

Outside by the Marrow's back exit, a carriage from the

palace is waiting for her, and within it, the general. Almost without her volition, she climbs in. The upholstery rasps against her skin like sandpaper. Perspiration pools at the base of her throat, behind her knees.

"Congratulations." Lussadh holds out a golden brooch. When Nuawa simply looks at it, unresponsive, the general frowns and reaches over to pin it under her collar. Hyacinth and snowflakes, as before. The queen's favorite flower, perhaps.

"To absolute winter, and to your grace," Nuawa says, mindlessly. Her mind is at once far away and inextricable from her skin. The sensation of being six. The carriage thrums as it sets into motion. She squeezes her eyes shut, forces herself to open them again. The rolling of wheels on road vibrates through her joints.

"Are you quite all right?"

She gazes at Lussadh's hand on her arm, a hot weight. "I will manage, General."

Lussadh doesn't seem persuaded, but she lets go. "I am glad that you made it. I don't like to bet on the wrong horse, so to speak."

"And if I make it through to the end, will I not be accused of doing so under the aegis of your favor rather than on my own strength?" Unwise to say, she realizes as she speaks, but her reason is lagging far behind her mouth.

"Not that I could have affected the results at this stage. But even if every step of the tournament had been broadcast in public, and the least citizens allowed to gawk in person, they would nevertheless say that of any winner. If you become my officer, you'll have to get used to being the subject of wild hearsay and speculation." Lussadh's eyes seem unusually huge in the sculpted frame of her face, jade-dark and lustrous. "How was it? I've never taken hallucinogens, certainly not ones which work like that."

"From the inside, it's very vivid." She fingers the brooch; it has not warmed to her skin, remains as frigid as icicles to her fingertip. "I felt the cold, heard the dark, and every contour of stone was brutishly real. It was an... experience."

The general is studying her closely, must notice the fever brilliance in Nuawa's eyes, the sheen of exertion. "I suspect I could ask you anything right now and you'd answer. Loosen your collar."

Nuawa does. Immediately her breathing eases, air entering her lungs properly, pure and cool. "Ask me then, General."

A faint smile. "Do you respect the opponents you took down?"

"Not particularly. Unsporting of me. I'm often chided for my deficit in sentiment and gallantry."

"What awaits them doesn't trouble you? I say this in confidence," Lussadh goes on, "but I do regret the process a little. They could have been useful infantry, probably, with some discipline."

"They chose to enter the games much as I did. Were our places exchanged they would waste no thought or pity on me." Sobriety is returning, fraction by fraction. "Each of us is motivated by ambition, avarice, ego, the need for fame: all the base and ignominious components, our hungry scavenging parts."

"And hunger is all we are, from the least of us to the greatest."

The carriage slows as it climbs the steep, winding path to the palace. They disembark at the gate. When Nuawa stumbles out, unsteady, the general catches her. "Let me," Lussadh says and, with little apparent strain, carries her into the entrance hall.

The attention they attract is immediate and undivided. Nuawa spots Governor Imnesh coming to a standstill, courtiers and diplomats pausing to stare, servants likewise. Not for long. Each moves on quickly, pretending this is nothing unusual. "If they didn't think you favored me unduly before, now they certainly would," she says flatly as they head toward their wing.

How Lussadh can keep to a brisk stride under this much weight she can't begin to guess. The general must be even stronger than she looks.

"I'm Her Majesty's second." The general's voice is dry. "I do what I like, duelist. Were you able to walk without assistance, I would leave you well enough alone."

Lussadh lets her down once they have reached Nuawa's suite. "Rest," the general says. "It'd be a shame for you to falter in the single combat segment after having survived this much."

Nuawa locks the door behind her. Despite her objections, she doubts she would have been able to make it here on her own. She falls into her bed, chilled by her own sweat, the oneiric glass bead still at her earlobe. She expects she will wake up weak and famished, mouth dry and joints aching.

She shuts her eyes and slips into the honeycomb underground, katabasis inevitable as the grave. The jagged rocks, the subtle indigo undercurrent in the black, the pallid quartz. Odors of soil and rot. Water drips, its thumping impact loud as footsteps. She is in command, fully conscious; she remembers that those she fought never woke up. This is the same arena and she hears them, wandering, lost. Perhaps still fighting even as their bodies are gathered for processing, believing that they've been given a second chance. Nuawa draws her gun, though her hand is sluggish, moving as if through sludge. The gold brooch is pinned over her heart, jostling for space against the silver.

Nuawa can almost feel the flow of antidote through her arteries, but though it sufficed to bring her to consciousness it hasn't —as it did the first time—purged her system of the dream-drug. She listens for noises, hears the slap of flesh on stone, and thinks back to her conversation with Lussadh. *What awaits them doesn't trouble you?*

It might have been her answer. It might have been something else, a thread of information plucked from the weave of her carefully curated background: whose daughter she truly is, what her mothers have done, tried to do. It could have been neither, merely a whim and impersonal cruelty. Either way, nearly nothing she does in here will change her immediate future. Or her future at all. Habit impels. She advances, footing cautious on wet stone. The air feels heavier, somehow, as though pressed down by the weight of the earth. If she must kill them all over again, she will. It will be menial, but it is a language in which her fluency is total.

"Absolute winter," she murmurs. The acoustics in this place do not obey physics and her voice comes back, too loud and too high. Like a voice about to crack, has cracked and rolled past into shrieking hysteria. Even now she might already be hauled out from her bed, unceremonious, deposited into a carriage that would bear her to a kiln.

She marches on.

Light ahead, jaundiced and unlovely. But humans are built to seek warmth and, in the absence of any other signal, she follows. It brightens, is soon no longer so dim, no longer a single ray into an oubliette. Forward into this annihilating bright until there is no more cavern. Not behind her, not above her, only the glare of a sun in zenith. It is incandescent, her skin feeling as though it will crisp and curl, paper in fire. Under her feet is sand and, in the distance, ruins leaning precarious on dunes the way old teeth cling—slanted, unsteady—to gums. This is a landscape which has never known the queen's touch, never come under her conquering gaze. The sky is cloudless and the horizons haze, warping into mirage.

"Nuawa Dasaret."

The faceless duelist is indistinct, even now, standing before her in all this light. Her hand twitches but she suppresses the urge to lift her gun and take aim. Their outline smudges and their mask is a perfect canvas, without features or contours.

"I believe I know what you are. This makes your placement interesting." Their voice is flat and toneless, without accent or indication of mood. When she doesn't answer the shape glides closer, the hem of its swaddling not quite touching the ground. Levitating. "You'll want to know who I am, but appreciate that such an answer is premature. I'll say that by approaching you at all, I have exposed myself. You are not in danger—your mortal coil is safe. This is only a passing fantasy."

Nuawa rubs at her skin. She imagines she can feel the fabric of the sheet, the comfort of the bed, her mind pushing its way up from hallucinogenic depths. "What do you think I am?"

"A weapon."

"Everyone is a weapon," she says. "Against an ideology; against themselves; against conditions that chew at existence. Even monks are weapons against earthly desire, honed to flense off lust and filed to puncture material need."

The mask flexes minutely. "Do you know what a mosquito is? No? They probably survive in the occident, but not in winter territories—too cold. Tiny insects with a taste for human blood. Their bites anesthetize; you don't feel it until long after they are sated and gone. They can infect you with a fatal fever that grinds apart your mind, unravels your body. As a species, we are mightier than any other animal, yet we fall to this, to pests and small terrors, the indignity of a single insect bite or stomach parasites."

A test, a game, something arbitrary. "You will have to be more specific."

"I know the Winter Queen's most essential desire, one she keeps secret even from her general, and I am in need of a weapon. If that is how you wish to spend yourself, then our goals may align. You have been receiving my messages. I can give you the resurrection of Vahatma, the god-engine that protected this city."

"Why would that be of interest to me?"

As though she has said nothing, the faceless creature goes on, "Where I came from we have living architecture, born from a seed of will and history. The core of your god-engine is not so different, and such seeds have been made with war in mind. Not easy to acquire—there are few left, the making of them now prohibited—but easier than plundering the queen's vaults to restore your god. What I ask of you will be little."

She doesn't push. They are loquacious, ready to persuade and coax, presenting what they have like a merchant coming to market. The longer she gazes at them, the more detail she can make out, impossibly superimposed onto the blank mask. Features in isolation: an eye heavily fringed with lashes, a nose marginally crooked. Each appears briefly and separately, does not come together to create an entire face.

"Lussadh al-Kattan left unfinished business, which falls to me to attend. The al-Kattans were purged thoroughly, the least branches and the most distant fruits. Kemiraj itself is a country of tradition. It respects lineage, and I have use for a scion of that dynasty."

Nuawa tightens her hand on the grip of her gun, for all that she realizes it would be pointless. They control the dream, not she. "Really."

The stranger cants their head. "To you it may seem outlandish, but it's a game I've been playing a long time. I know its board, its moves. All I need is a certain piece."

"And I have the compatible anatomy, I suppose." It is astonishing, the idea. Several occidental countries are similarly monarchic, similarly obsessed with heritage, but even so. "You expect me to seduce the general, conceive her child, and what—raise it to be a Kemiraj heir for you to use?"

A mouth moves beneath the mask, stretching impossibly. "You will not have to rear the child. It is merely a matter of transferring the unborn babe to a womb of resin or stone, or cold iron if you prefer. That would be the extent of our transaction."

"What if I develop maternal fondness and refuse to be extricated?"

The smile widens. "That seems unlikely."

She doesn't press the point; she can't picture herself seized by tenderness either, a spontaneous fever, a madness of the spirit. At any stage of pregnancy, should she ever fall into it the way one falls into a sinkhole. "You claim to know the queen's secret."

"Hard-won. I would be amenable to sharing it with allies, in due time."

"Suppose I agree to it." She has no intention of doing so. "How do you propose to track my progress? Have someone press their ear to the general's wall?"

"You sneer, but that is how it was done in a time when machine-wombs were a dream and children were born from the flesh alone. Primitive, but it did work for its time. I'm not interested in the sordid particulars. Let's say a deadline. In one month, the tournament will have finished and you'll have won — consider your victory a fringe benefit of my friendship — and by then you should have what I want. I will know of whose blood it is."

A knot of seed and ovum, embryonic, incubated within her and then drawn out like pus. "And that would be all."

"That would be all."

Simple, tidy. Nothing to it — *That would be all.* She imagines saying that to Lussadh. A convoluted delusion, as delusional as the thought of resurrecting the god-engine Vahatma.

The desert dissolves, and Nuawa is back in the bed, thick furs and pastel sheets on her like snowdrift. Her mouth is parched and after-images of the pitiless sky linger, igniting the edge of her vision. The room is otherwise dark; outside it must be past sunset.

Delicately, she takes off the glass bead. Considers crushing it underfoot or throwing it out the window. In the end, she seals it inside a pouch. When she falls into natural sleep, it is to the desert that she returns, as long and wide as a tundra, endless, washed out in gold.

NINE

THE HARD PERCUSSION OF HAIL ON ROOF IS LOUD IN THE engine-shrine, the palace's highest point. Lussadh waits for the viper locks to reknit themselves, barring the door once more, before she calls on the queen. Not the most auspicious of places to contact Her Majesty, but it is the most insulated and best protected. When the queen answers, she says, "My apologies for calling you from here. It was the most private place I could think of." She doesn't say that her own suite no longer feels so after another failed attempt to locate and bring Ytoba to heel. She is standing by the shuttered window, facing away from the engine's shell, but even so the image of it is inescapable. In this shrine Vahatma is written everywhere, its name into the floor tiles, its images etched into the walls and painted on the ceiling.

"It is nothing." The queen manifests at quarter-self, her substance transparent, the fabrics on her all gossamer. Her eyes are leeched gray in this light. She looks over her shoulder at what remains of Vahatma, its empty elegant husk. "Had it offended me, I'd have had it destroyed when I took this city. I allow it to remain, for this is a symbol of Sirapirat's defeat. They used to pray to it for vengeance, for my destruction, but not anymore. You're distracted. Are the games not going to your liking?"

"No, my queen. Rather the opposite. I have a candidate — I'm almost certain she is a glass-bearer, and she's winning. No others have presented themselves, and I've made certain to meet every contestant at least once."

Her Majesty's smile is quick. "I shall be there for the finals, and much look forward to seeing this person who has so captivated you. No, I know you well, my own heart. And I know my mirror. It compels pieces of itself to one another. Like beckons to like, in lust and otherwise."

Lussadh studies the mural of Vahatma's tranquil aspect descending upon a stormy sea. Done in deep colors with the god a lone spot of brilliance, platinum corona against the black of roiling tides. "That's not what preoccupies me, no. It's a personal matter, my queen. Beneath your attention."

"When it concerns you, it is never beneath my attention."

"Minor trouble from Kemiraj." The balance between forthrightness and showing no fear. What would she be if she cannot resolve this on her own and must run to her queen like a cringing child. "Nothing I cannot handle, Your Majesty. I'm in no danger."

"You've served me with faith and tireless diligence, and ruthless efficiency," the queen murmurs. "If you require my aid, I'll never think less of you. This you must know, my treasure. My best treasure."

She kisses the queen's hand; it is as soft and white as a new lily. "I will count the minutes until I see you again in the flesh."

Leaving the shrine, she wonders whether the queen *could* crush Ytoba, just like that. The queen has explained once that winter is part of her; wherever the chill penetrates, she is present in some measure. Not omniscient, but close. The mirror would have been her eyes, when it was whole. *As you must be my eyes and ears,* said of her glass-bearers and her general especially.

But even Lussadh does not know the full extent of the queen's reach.

Ulamat is waiting for her in the indoor garden, an area of rose-quartz fountains and pots of water lilies. Shadow-curtains pendulate from the ceiling, their shades chasing sunrise colors, peach-gold and copper. Low, flat benches and round tables that bear game-boards: chance and strategy, pawns and tokens and cards. Her aide is dressed blandly, between a clerk and a menial, and kneels among the faceted pots. At first glance he could easily be mistaken for a gardener. Part practice, part natural chameleon.

"This will be sudden, but I need you on another task," she says briskly. "The duelist I have a handle on. This other matter — you are to find a Kemiraj person in their sixties." Ytoba's gift for obfuscating eir appearance is not total, and must obey the limits of their natural physique. And it is a wasted, ruined physique, unless ey has found a miracle. Nor can ey assume more than one guise in a month. "Likely frail, certainly scarred, if not on the face then the body. The scars could appear as the result of a burn, blade, or even port-wine stain. Ten centimeters shorter than I am, much slighter."

"My *lord*."

"Not an easy person to find," she grants. "But if anyone can, it would be you."

He pulls at a blade of grass, wincing when it comes free. "How dangerous is this person, lord?"

"Extremely. You are to never engage them. Use what agent you can, always at a remove. Eir name is Ytoba, and ey used to serve my family as an assassin. Back then there were no walls ey could not penetrate, no defense ey could not bypass. Ey is much diminished today, though still incredibly lethal." And should not be alive at all.

Ulamat's mouth tightens. Remembering, perhaps, what life

was like in Kemiraj for his people. "If my lord says she has the duelist well in hand, then she does. I'll do my utmost."

"Without endangering yourself."

"Of course not, my lord." He dips his head. "I'm glad to be of use."

Lussadh watches him go and wonders whether she's misjudged—whether he might make a reckless play for Ytoba after all, whether she will send him to his death. But of her people he is the one to whom this can be entrusted, the one suited to the hunt. The one with a vendetta against a representative of Kemiraj-that-was. He knows better than to spend his life, she must trust that. He knows the worth of that particular currency more precisely than any other.

Once he is out of sight, she says, "I know you are there. Why not come out and get it over with?"

The assassin is not there—though she has heard their breathing—and then is, materializing as though out of nothing but fountain spray and rose-quartz gleam. Their head is hidden behind a mesh of moth wings and pulsating tendons, eyes and nose and mouth invisible entirely. A belt of shark-blades. Not Ytoba; different stance, different style, and too obvious. Ytoba would have been a thin shadow, one she wouldn't have seen or heard coming.

A blur of limbs and shark-knives. Her gun is in her hand, already vibrating with the pressure of ammunition. It requires no aiming; she pulls the trigger.

The frost-bees block out the sound of hailstones, their droning almost physical in force, the chill they radiate a fraction of the queen's—but it is enough to, momentarily, turn the room arctic. She sees the assassin slow; sees the assassin fling their hands up to shield their face, to little success. The bees blanket them in white, a burial sheet. Even the mask of moth and sinew is scant protection. Death by venom or suffocation is death all the same.

The swarm subsides, some of them falling apart to component icicles, others drifting sluggish and sated back into the muzzle. It is not an easy ammunition to control and she is pleasantly surprised to discover the assassin alive. The dead cannot be interrogated, after all. She removes the helm, moth wings tickling her fingers. An eye dangles loosely on its stem, excavated from its socket by a particularly inquisitive bee. The nose and mouth are red, swollen, but they are breathing. She sends for the lieutenant.

She hears the shark-blades susurrate behind her. Then a single, ringing shot. Conventional bullet meeting metal animus. The glassy ligament that holds the belt together breaks and the blades fall to the quartz floor, clanking.

Nuawa advances through the door, gun pointed at the belt. "General," she says mildly. "You are unharmed?"

"Quite." Lussadh glances at the inert shark-blades. "My thanks. You're timely."

"There was a great deal of noise, mostly the bees." The duelist is fresh from the Marrow, the musk of exertion still on her. Drenched head to foot, dripping from rain and melted hail. She slowly holsters her gun.

The lieutenant arrives. "Have them interrogated," Lussadh murmurs. "Report to me by evening." To Nuawa she says, "Let us get you warm and dry before you catch your death."

In the bath, as in her suite, she has strung up more of the frost-spiders until the ceiling glitters white. They don't do well here; close to heat, none of the queen's tools or gifts do, but they are not entirely useless.

Nuawa stands apart from her as she turns the valves and waits for the ghosts to cook the pipes. "You don't have to,

General, and your personnel won't be happy. Even I could be a security risk."

"Fear is the assassin's first weapon." Lussadh pulls two robes from the rack, holding one out to the duelist. "Destabilize the target and much of the battle is already won. I'd make mistakes, scared of my own shadow. In any case that wasn't the most adept of killers, badly armed and I knew they were there well in advance. You pose a greater threat than they, certainly."

The duelist does not quite smile. Hers is not an expression that lends itself to mirth, Lussadh suspects. "In a fight against you, I wouldn't bet on myself." She undoes her hair, starts to unbutton her jacket. "We've got a public bath at the Marrow, but I worry for your sense of propriety."

This is said in the same tone as *There was a great deal of noise.* Polite, factual. "My sense of propriety has survived much worse," she says. "Make yourself comfortable. Wear those robes, or not."

They clean themselves in the shower partition; Lussadh, out first, listens to the running water and puts on a robe. When she emerges, the duelist is wearing hers knotted around her waist, contemptuous of its capability to cover or contemptuous of the idea of modesty. Her hair is down, wet and sudsy. Two sets of scars on her belly, as of laceration made by claws, stopping just below her breasts.

"Where did you get those from?" Lussadh takes a pumice stone from its sconce.

The duelist presents her back. "When I was young, I used to hunt. Bears, wolves."

Nuawa's shoulders are narrower than Lussadh thought, her upper body slimmer, the structure of her bones built as though for someone more delicate. She lathers up the soap in her hands until it is a thick froth and sweeps the duelist's hair out of the way. "A hobby? Somehow I don't think you hunted them for the hide or the meat."

"I did. But no, it wasn't strictly necessary."

Lussadh spreads the lather down, from Nuawa's neck to the small of her back. Dense, hard muscles. A knot of scar tissue near her right shoulder blade but the duelist's skin is supple otherwise, few blemishes. "Do you consider it a sport then, fighting? The act of it, the concept." She studies Nuawa's ear, the convoluted seashell of cartilage, the earlobe.

"To me, it's work like any other. Hard labor. There's no art to it, and I don't think of it as a sport. I have a suitable disposition, that is all. Had I one more suited to carpentry, I would have pursued carpentry. Or painting, or pottery. It's not a profession I took up out of love or passion."

"And you take no pride."

Nuawa leans forward, letting Lussadh scrub down the length of her spine. She is pale the way some of Sirapirat natives can be, a little like the queen but with a subtle undertone of warm gold rather than glacier blue. "Maybe I do a little. What about you, General? What do you take pleasure in?"

If this is suggestive, again there is no telltale sign. Lussadh inhales. The steam is thickening, heady. She pours water over Nuawa, rinsing away the soap. "In the same things as anyone else. Excellent food, a hot bath, the company of good friends. Since I'm enjoying two out of three, I would say this is a better day than most."

The duelist meets Lussadh's eyes over her shoulder. "I didn't think you would consider me a friend."

"For one, you haven't tried to kill me; for another, you are intriguing. These are two of the qualities I prize. Make of that what you will."

The duelist's lips twitch, her eyes widening slightly. "You aren't being very subtle."

"Being a soldier, I prefer to be direct. Leave the rest to diplomats."

Nuawa studies her, attention like a weight. It is not often

Lussadh feels herself the subject of such, being considered, even judged. Something tips the scale. Nuawa reaches backward to untie Lussadh's robe, pulling the sash off. A surprised laugh. "You're hard already, General." Nuawa's fingers glide, touch.

"Let me see if that is mutual," Lussadh says against the tender skin at the duelist's throat. When she cups Nuawa's breast in her hand, she finds the nipple stiff. She circles it slowly with her thumb. "Tell me what you like."

"Use your teeth." Nuawa lets out a sigh, soft, when Lussadh bites—tentative, then decisive. "Yes."

Lussadh quickly learns the topography of Nuawa's nerve-ends, where she is sensitive, where she responds. The duelist answers the pressure of teeth, the bite of nails, with small reflexive movements. She is a quiet partner, quiet as she takes Lussadh's cock into her mouth. Her tongue is deft, firm. Lussadh shuts her eyes. Grips the sides of Nuawa's head and says, "Wait."

She lifts Nuawa onto her lap. The duelist's legs curl around her waist. The rest is repetitive rhythm and pressure, Nuawa craning her head back—the cords in her throat compelling Lussadh to kiss them again, bite once more, hard enough to bruise—the duelist makes short, sharp sounds like prayer. Their bodies heave. Incredible heat, the floor cool beneath them.

In Lussadh's coral bed, the duelist lies on her back, eyes wide open as though bemused at where she is and what she has been doing. Lussadh turns on the heating and listens to the ghosts murmur, a low purr that thrums through walls and ebony boards. Shamans—alchemists of the spirit—can hear and understand their chatter, it is said, the secrets of the dead. If that is so she expects it is mostly banal; some ghosts believing themselves alive, going through their daily matters the same as they did in life. Chores, routines. The afterlife through the queen's kilns is an amnesiac's dream, full of forgetting.

From the corner of her eye she glances at the duelist. "I

thought you'd go to your own room," she says. "Not that I'm complaining."

"You said you had a bigger bed." Nuawa holds up a fistful of green silk, turning it this way and that. She plucks at a length of ermine, experimentally draping it over her chest, running her hand over the fur. "The room smells of you. I like that you don't use perfume."

"I use some scented oils, but with a very light hand. I find most perfumes too obtrusive. Even colognes I can't bear at all." Warmth radiates—too high. She adjusts the dials, more self-conscious than she would like to admit. It *has* been a long time since she shared a private space with anyone, in this capacity. "Something to drink?"

"I'd rather be sober. Or get no drunker than I already am."

The implied compliment—*you intoxicate me*—is somehow absent in the way Nuawa says it. Is it misgiving, Lussadh wonders, the decision to plunge into what was once safe to indulge at the Filament House. The actual thing after the play, and how it measures up. She tries to picture what that was like, whether this Kemiraj courtesan resembles her in any significant way. The face in profile. The shape and build of the body. A former dynastic subject, technically. Perhaps now a citizen registered to Sirapirat. "Regretting this already?"

The duelist rolls onto her stomach, propping her head in her hands. "Merely alarmed at myself. I suppose it'd ruin the mood to say that in the final tribute, if I lose I would be sent to the machines, like any other."

The plea to intercede then, but Lussadh didn't take Nuawa for that sort. Nor does it sound like one. "Are you afraid?"

Half a smile. "I've watched all the rounds. I've measured my competition. No, I'm not afraid. Nevertheless the fact is there, the possibility. I couldn't have chosen a worse time. But you invited, and I was curious and couldn't be sure you would repeat the invitation."

Lussadh sits on the bed, the mattress bending under her. She draws a line from the back of Nuawa's knee, up the curve of buttock. Firm, like the rest of the duelist. "You can pretend this never happened. I'm fastidious with contraceptives."

"So am I. No, that was fine. Were the timing less portentous —" Nuawa splays her fingers on Lussadh's thigh, stops short of touching. "Perhaps when all is done, you could reward me personally."

"When all is done," Lussadh agrees and takes Nuawa's hand, brushing her lips across the duelist's knuckles one by one.

TEN

NUAWA DOES NOT SPEND THE NIGHT IN LUSSADH'S BED. IT seems faintly obscene to play at intimacy, unduly needy; she cannot imagine herself in the general's arms, falling asleep to the general's breathing, waking up to the same. She thinks back, inevitably compares. Somehow the make-believe at the Filament House was *more*. She had thought this, a culmination of danger and attraction, would overwhelm and annihilate. That it would leave her skin raw and her thoughts in disarray. She may have expected too much. She is still herself, contained and absolute.

She rinses her mouth and examines herself, touching where the general has touched, and finds to her satisfaction that nothing in her has altered. Not even inside, for if Kemiraj is as mad for heritage as the oneirologist claims, Lussadh would have every reason to keep herself infertile and make sure none of her seed goes to fruit however unlikely the soil. Fastidious use of contraceptives. The thought of conceiving, bearing that embryo. How mad, how bizarre.

At dawn, she takes her morning walk around the palace grounds. Palace sentries watch her, faceless behind their frost-and-iron masks, living statues in images of the queen. Once or twice she considers venturing near Vahatma's shrine, those serpent-locked doors, but decides against it. Instead she loiters by the gate, waiting for it to open.

The directions Yifen gave her were derived partly from gossip—piecing together rumors from the Marrow as to the oneirologist's identity and whereabouts—and partly from divination. Yifen does not admit to being a practitioner, but her work with the glass bead looked effortless and the result is pinpoint. The old observatory sits atop a hill that overlooks Wat Totsanee, belonging to an era where nighttime in Sirapirat was unlit, now four decades out of use. Some issue of land ownership has stopped it from being converted or demolished, so it sits derelict, a playground for children to venture at night on a dare.

In the morning glow it looks worn, unthreatening. A domed cylinder, formerly the tallest building in the city, that status since usurped by university buildings, the chedi at Wat Wansanoj, and the palace's extensions. The façade was once burgundy or rust-red; the paint has peeled in patches, gone gray, some of it covered by graffiti. One is of a mermaid, scaled skin chartreuse and hair full of sea-serpents, limbs heavy with anglerfish.

Its closest neighbor is a store selling condiments in jars and cheap toiletries and carpentry tools. Nuawa makes her way from that, scaling the bitumen roof. There is no convenient balcony, this being one of the truly traditional houses, renovated for insulation and ghost pipes but retaining its native architecture. All Sirapirat, treated wood and obtuse angles. She makes the leap, lands lightly by the dome. For precarious seconds she hangs from the eave, tendons at war with gravity, muscles performing stunning alchemy. When she pulls herself up, clinging arachnid to a window, she paces her breathing. Exertion is its own ecstasy, the human engine rewarding itself.

She shuts the window behind her, the hinge wobbly from her entry. The observatory's uppermost chamber smells of damp and dust, littered by the skeleton of astronomic equipment, the base

of an absent telescope. The iron mezzanine is surprisingly solid
and whole after all this time. There is no sign of habitation save a
house shrine, new and painted white, housing several icons: a
deer-hooved girl she doesn't recognize, the garuda god Yuthram.
But this may not be the oneirologist—who must be foreign in
any case—so much as nearby residents. Every building needs its
small gods, especially one as venerable and abandoned as this.

Not much to see otherwise, nor did she expect to. This is a
person who treads lightly and displays few possessions, not even
the paraphernalia of oneirology or alchemy. Perhaps they keep
their atelier elsewhere, corkscrew glassware and wire-mesh
orrery, bottled evanescence and fresh ghosts. Ghosts, the everything medium, multipurpose—engine fuel, dreams, specialized
miracles. Most express utility in death that they never did in life.
Easy to grasp and even embrace the queen's logic, her mass
conversion of bodies to ghost, the compost heaps of the afterlife.
What are a few tragedies, next to that.

Nuawa settles by a rust-eaten worktable, out of the line of
sight from either window or the stair leading up from the ground
level, positioning herself so she'd see anyone entering through
both. Contract work has endowed her with a certain expertise, a
bounty of patience. Not beyond possibility that the oneirologist
has spooked, but she has time.

Below, hinges creak. The corrugated door swings inward.
She watches and knows at once this must be the oneirologist.
They look no threat. Stringy meat on bent bone, stripped down
as carrion picked clean, a burned face. Her mind leaps to a
certain association—her own preoccupations of late, the courtesan—and at once recognizes the cast and glaze of them, the
stem of their making. The Kemiraj look, to which she is hyper-
vigilant. Normally such a look signifies nothing. At this moment,
it signifies all.

Something gives her away, a disturbance in the air or a slant
of light. The oneirologist looks up. Nuawa fires almost at once

but they are already running, the door clanging shut. She swears, knowing as she does that it is wasted breath, and yanks the window open. Her descent is fast, reckless, and will be too late even so. She doesn't climb—she makes calculated drops, and by the time her feet are on the ground she is out of breath, teeth and bones vibrating from impact.

When she dashes around to the observatory's entrance, she finds the oneirologist down, at gunpoint. She stops short. The man holding the gun is vaguely familiar, in the way a face she's seen in a crowd multiple times might be. From the palace. "I work for the general," he says quickly, though his aim doesn't waver.

In any other circumstances, she would not have taken him at his word. She approaches, slow, her own pistol out. The oneirologist is bleeding from their shin, a well-placed disabling shot. She wonders whether they were once a bureaucrat or courtier; her knowledge of the empire is thin. Two continents away after all, entirely deposed and carefully blotted. The Kemiraj of today bears little resemblance to its past and unlike in Sirapirat, she hears that its citizens are encouraged to forget. Most subjects of winter are. She imagines that this seared, stooped husk was a creature of politics, fostering schemes and game-pieces, every step ringing with ambition.

"Who were you?" she asks softly. The features she saw in the dream, now in the flesh and unmasked. One eye with thick lashes, the other not at all, consigned to the fire that took half their face and neck. It doesn't look like an injury sustained in combat, rather something much more surgical. Punishment, revenge.

Their mouth stretches. It is a rictus. In a face so wracked it can be nothing else. "What I was bears no relevance. You'll learn soon enough." In the dream, their voice was as frictionless as quicksilver; in person it is as ruined as the rest of them, creaking with age and damage. "You've reneged on our bargain."

"I never agreed to it, I fear."

Their head twitches as they try to pull upright. But whatever they mean to do, they fall back, resigned perhaps. Their eyes clench shut. To the side, the general's man is speaking rapidly into his calling-glass.

Nuawa has been waiting close to an hour in the indoor garden before Lussadh appears. In the meantime, she observes the diplomats and their staff with anthropological interest. She doesn't come into frequent contact with foreigners, let alone this particular subset, those elevated in their own lands. A handful of women in dresses of varying eccentricity: occidental costumes with stiff hoop skirts, an islander's saturated colors adapted for the cold. Bodyguards, though they aren't allowed firearms on palace premises.

When the general comes they vacate the garden, though they have the presence of mind to pay respect first. It is fascinating to see the occidentals variously address Lussadh as a man or a woman when the general is neither; the islanders acquit themselves better, eliding the general's gender entirely in their courtesy.

Lussadh's sleeves are flecked with red, brown stains. At Nuawa's look, the general rolls them back, an appearance of cleanness hiding what she must have just done: the needle and the tongs, the scalpels. "That got messy," she says. "Ytoba isn't an easy person to converse with. Ey used to serve as an assassin. A long time ago. When I was young, I would never have imagined em brought low in defeat. But I wasn't able to imagine a lot of things."

"You're tired, General." She takes Lussadh's hand, drawing her down to sit at the fountain's edge. The water is still for the moment, surface tension hardening to rime.

"Not exactly." The general passes her hand over her eyes then shakes herself, as though to throw her fatigue off. "Ytoba's changed a great deal. Taking up oneirology was as logical a choice as any, I suppose. There's a person who lives for an idea of the past, not even any specific person—my grandaunt—but the idea of the throne, the dynasty. The crown and scepter, the sword and the executioner's axe. You've done me a considerable favor, a great service to winter."

"The credit is more to your aide than anything. He was the one who followed me and made that shot."

"Hah." Lussadh tests the fountain; the rime crackles and breaks. Underneath the water is tinged silver, the rose-quartz bottom gleaming with coins. Most are foreign, triangular or seashell, cubic and cylindrical. Stamped with heads of state distant or centuries buried, or heraldic animals. "You would disdain a medal or two, I expect. Were this the country of my birth, the king would have given you a tract of land or a lucrative trade commission, and likely an aristocratic spouse of your choice."

Nuawa raises an eyebrow. "Or the hand of her grandniece the prince?"

"Not quite that far. In retrospect it was all quite mad, our system, the arbitrariness of it. The way people raptly listened at doors to make sure this embodiment of one lineage is copulating —and reproducing—with one of another lineage. All that. I'm not sure how Kemiraj could run the way it was for that long, one generation after the next bowing its head and accepting ... that as the rightful order." A grimace. "My apologies. I ramble. Your last match is in what, two days?"

Her opponent being an ex-soldier, a veteran once in Lussadh's service, though the general doesn't appear to have taken notice, or particularly care. A nobody, Nuawa surmises. "So it is."

"What bargain did Ytoba try to strike with you, anyway?"

"A plot that struck me as mad," Nuawa says without missing a beat. "Ey wanted me to bear your child that ey would then, I was given to understand, utilize in some scheme. Ey didn't specify what."

Lussadh looks at her and makes an abortive laugh. "*Is* that why you slept with me?"

"That would make no sense. Both you and I use contraceptives, for one. Or perhaps you were so good in bed that I changed my mind and sought to bring down Ytoba rather than participate in a plot I don't actually understand."

"You're very difficult."

"I try." Nuawa does not quite kiss the general; she licks around Lussadh's lips, tasting the remnant of red tea and pomegranate. Lussadh tugs at her clothes, one hand snaking under jacket and shirt. It is tempting. Nuawa moves against the general's hand, rubbing her nipple on those calluses, picturing herself bent over the fountain—face centimeters from icy water, straining for balance, gasping Lussadh's name one sibilant syllable at a time as the general leaves teeth prints on her neck, her shoulder. The angle, the friction. She could be loud and pleading, and the general would never think to ask what precisely it was that Ytoba promised her in recompense.

A percussive rhythm begins, in the distance.

"*Fuck,*" Lussadh gasps, harsh and breathless. "This timing. Fuck. I'm sorry. I need to go to her."

Nuawa extricates herself. Makes a shallow bow. "Of course, General."

She buttons up her shirt, tidies up her belt and trousers, and strides to the window. Her cheeks are flushed, not that there is anyone to see, for which she is glad. The drumming continues; it is known through all of winter, a composition played for one occasion and one only. The gongs first, struck one after another from the palace's rooftops, then drums and keen flute notes in crescendo. Every palace, however remote or distant from the capital, has musicians on hand who can play it, and the requisite instruments. It is not the first time Nuawa has heard this music. To her it has always sounded funereal and opprobrious. In a remote country, that sealed-off Yatpun, it might be the song of empire.

Below, on the sloping path to the palace, the Winter Queen walks. No escort, though she is armored, the same set she wore to Nuawa's execution all those years ago. The same coronet cupping her skull and her hair like the tail of a black comet. Stone and soil freeze where she treads and behind her, ice glimmers, a jagged diamantine train. The palace's red-gold gate has been thrown wide. In all the breadth and width of her empire, no door—however private, however holy—may remain shut to the queen.

General Lussadh has appeared on bended knee, head down in obeisance. The gongs resound one last time, conclusive, and fall silent.

ELEVEN

THE HOUSE IS NOTHING SPECIAL TO LOOK AT, THE MARKS OF A comfortable life and quiet wealth: the lawn is tidy, the walls are high but not forbidding. There is a greenhouse fogged over, the inside of it perspiring and fruitful, and empty trellises in what could have been a garden in warmer times. It is located apart from the nearest collection of farmsteads and orchards, away from the roads, the house of someone private. Tall evergreens shield it from immediate view. There are no guards or defenses, nor any sign of danger or suspicious matter.

Lussadh has come alone. The back of her throat is sour; even now she is not sure what Ytoba—who successfully asked audience of the queen—said to persuade Her Majesty to send Lussadh here. Petty revenge against Nuawa. Faintly, treasonously, she hopes that the house will be empty; that Nuawa's aunt has been forewarned, or is out running errands. But when she rings the door, it is promptly answered. Not by a servant.

Indrahi Dasaret is a small woman, shorter than her niece, in her fifties or sixties. Though she looks soft, not a trained combatant, she bears her age with dignity. Her posture is excellent; this is someone who has been tutored in etiquette and comportment.

When she takes in Lussadh there is the slightest recoil of surprise, but it is quickly subsumed. The woman curtsies deeply. "General Lussadh al-Kattan. Your presence graces this house as the stars grace a night sky."

"Citizen," Lussadh says, is at a loss what to add next. *I'm here to arrest you* seems uncivil. *I'm here to arrest you for no reason I can discern* is worse. "You are Nuawa Dasaret's aunt and guardian, I've been led to understand."

"She's an adult, which makes my status as guardian obsolete. But yes, I did raise her, if that is what you mean. I trust she hasn't been giving anyone trouble?" Said mildly, reproachfully, like a concerned parent.

"Not at all."

"Please come in, General. I'd be a poor citizen to keep you out on the veranda."

The drawing room is well-furnished, tasteful, nothing remarkable in it save the diptych that takes up most of one wall. It is vivid and must have been expertly preserved, either through mechanical or thaumaturgical means. The paint looks as if it could have just dried minutes ago, the blue of a sky so vivid it could have belonged to Kemiraj, the dashes of birds in flight keenly alive. A gilded sun, a river, flowers. Simple, of a realist style Lussadh does not recognize, and ultimately banal. Not even seditious—it is no image of bonfires or of winter giving way to spring. "How is Nuawa?" the aunt is asking. "I haven't heard much from her. In the way of family, we don't always get along."

Lussadh wonders if that is a thinly veiled barb. In the way of family. "You know of her work?"

"I know of her work and that you invited her to stay at the palace. Rumors travel fast, General, and idle old women like myself read gossip sheets on occasion."

She doubts that, though the drawing room evinces no suggestion of Indrahi's taste or intellectual character. The only book is a volume of scripture, biding dusty and thick next to an empty celadon vase. Now that she thinks of it, she can't remember the last time she met with a lover's parent. Most who have come to her bed did not do so with expectations of a lasting affair, let alone anything that would involve the formality of familial intro- duction. Absurd to contemplate that now. It is not as if she will ask this woman for Nuawa's hand. "She is well." Trite to say, empty of meaning. "She's acquitted herself admirably."

Indrahi lifts the lid from a tray on her table; underneath, persimmons and papayas, a stray orange. Each the bright yellow and red of pyres. She peels the orange, separates the segments neatly. "You mean in the arena, I assume. She's always been good at what she chooses to pursue. She doesn't often visit. So it goes with children who have left their roosts. Do you have any, General?"

"No." Lussadh has always made sure. Back in her former life, she held the informal—and sordid—duty of tracking down cousins' offshoots, an irresponsible uncle or aunt, curbing the diluted and illegitimate branches of the dynasty. "I wouldn't make much of a parent, let alone a good one. Rearing a child seems like a precarious venture." Even if, as with Kemiraj royals, speech and behavior are instilled pre-birth. Language and ritual woven into the artificial womb. Not a process often done anymore, though she can access it, the privilege of a governor.

"It's an interesting venture. Like performing complex surgery on yourself. You learn so much about your own character in the process." Nuawa's aunt gestures at the fruits. "I don't suppose you'd care for any of these? I grew the persimmons myself and can attest to their pedigree. No? Some want their children to become an idealized version of themselves, or lead lives that passed them by. Others want children as a sort of pet, affection on demand—for that a dog is superior, and much cheaper to bring up. Then there are those who come to parenthood by sheer, abrupt accident. For most of my life, I didn't think myself a likely parent either."

"What changed your mind?" Lussadh continues to study the woman. Nothing about her seems like a threat, not her bearing or build. Unarmed, almost certainly. Not much of a family resemblance.

"Well, Nuawa's mother dying, for one. I adopted her when she was eight, a solemn child from the beginning. Dutiful, not precisely what you'd call loving. I gave her the best of what I could afford, food and learning and clothing." She cuts the persimmon into thin slices. "And I was hoping she would take up a normal, proper vocation. I could have paid for her apprenticeship to a printer, a jeweler, or even to pursue a field of her choice at the university. But here we are. A common fighter, as if she had need to commodify her body."

"Citizen," Lussadh says, defensive of the duelist in spite of herself, "I'm a soldier."

"Surely. But that is different. What you do is important to winter's reach and reign. What my niece does, sadly, is entertainment for the rich. She lines her manager's pockets and not much else. It is," Indrahi says, shaking her head, "all hopeless."

Odd to think of Nuawa so contained in herself, graceful, assured next to this. The way the parent reduces the child. She is not unaccustomed to it; has witnessed such of her own kin, back then. "She will become one of my soldiers, in all likelihood. Most parents would derive some pride from that. Indeed the highest pride."

"Will she? Ah—the tournament. Yes." One more slice of persimmon disappears into Indrahi's mouth. A drop of translucent juice clings to her finger, the color of jaundice. "That will be an incredible honor. I have every hope that she will serve you well, for she's unlikely to find a respectable career anywhere else."

She begins to see why Nuawa might not often visit her aunt. Perhaps this will not be so difficult, after all, and Ytoba's revenge has been misaimed. "I share your hope, citizen. For the moment, would you come with me? It's nothing," she adds. "Call it an interview, if you would, as you're the immediate kin of someone who will soon be sworn in to the army."

Something passes through Indrahi's expression; Lussadh has the impression, for a moment, that Nuawa's aunt has been expecting this. "Let me finish eating this," Indrahi murmurs. "I hate wasting food. And when you see Nuawa, remind her to pick up that diptych, will you?"

———

At the Marrow, Tezem has sent their best, a splendor of regard in accoutrements, a retinue of attendants. The clothes provided for her are in winter colors, the gleam and the glare. Lustrous gray, pearl white, dashes of indigo. A resin mask painted like a glacier. Nuawa dons it all without objection, good practice for the near future. The previous rounds have been almost nondescript. This one will have all the theater each duelist's sponsors can marshal.

In the fifteen minutes allotted to her to prepare, she thinks of nothing in particular and utters no prayer. As with anywhere else, the result is between her and her circumstances. She has never thought much of divine intervention. Were the gods so merciful and appreciative of the offerings they receive in Sirapirat, she would like to think winter would never have come. A childish response, some theologians would say; beside the point, the monks would insist. To her, it is merely practical. Gods that do not answer or act are of less use than ghosts in the pipes.

The bell sounds; the arena gate lifts. The obsidian dome, the agate tiles. All routine. Her second home.

Ghost combustion fills the arena with arctic light, illuminating her and her opponent, amplifying their shadows to monstrous size. The ex-soldier has been costumed too, a crow-like affair, dark clothes and velvet tatters woven into their hair. A mask like hers, modeled after the queen's soldiers. Blue-black, the colors of tundra and frozen rivers. He is svelte but the costume adds the illusion of bulk. The way a cobra's hood flares to intimidate, and because Nuawa is as animal as any other human, it subtly works. They draw their swords in simpatico. His is serrated, verdantly serpentine. He bears no firearm. Nuawa's blade throws just two shadows today but they are sharkish, elongated by the light, bristling with thorns and teeth.

A warping of air, a fragmentation of movement: his shadow abruptly eclipses hers. Nuawa defends in time, metal screeching on metal. Point-blank she shoots. The bullet breaks into a constellation of shrapnel. He staggers back—a line of blood, in fine spray.

They regard each other. His heart, she imagines, hammers in his throat. She was forthright when she told Lussadh that she doesn't enjoy the pursuit of battle, that it is hard labor, one that happens to suit her. But there is satisfaction to be found in the calculation for survival, in totting it up correctly and seizing the sum. A mathematician's joy, delirious, potent. Down to who can solve the equation of combat first, and how fast.

He strikes quickly and with force, to stop her from firing again. A superior swordsman. Each blow jolts her to the shoulder, to her clenched teeth, makes her wrist sing. She gets another shot off, one that should have caught him full in the knee; it merely grazes. She gives ground, and gives ground again, holstering her gun to fight two-handed. Her blade-shadows lash and snap at his feet, never quite catching him.

His breathing is loud, louder than it should be, close to hyperventilation. The fringe benefit of Ytoba's friendship. Each dose of dream drugs carried something extra, something that wasn't added to hers. The Kemiraj assassin must have singled her out ever since the second round, at the latest.

She suffers the shallow cuts, the bruising impact. The costume is no armor, for her or him. The tip of her blade rakes down his sleeve, splitting it, opening the skin. The edge of his comes close to taking off her arm. She counts the seconds, measuring against previous fights, against her own endurance. Whether she could defeat him in a perfectly fair fight is immaterial. Some factor—vagaries of the body, of the arena, of the day— would always interfere with the computation. *Now* is the sole reference point that holds pertinence.

The ex-soldier is slowing down, nearly imperceptibly. The most minute of delay in his response. Still deadly. In a different time, he might have downed her.

Such things are decided within the span of a heartbeat, within the snap of seconds.

He advances, too far, mistiming his momentum. She grabs his wrist, wrenches him forward—he feels light as paper, as light as leaves—and brings her blade down. Across his shoulder blade, down to the back of his hip. The blade-shadows tear into him, the rip of whetted ether on flesh, on soul.

He falls. She trains her gun on him, even so, as the pool of his hemorrhage spreads and runs into the tiles, as the stink of it rises. She didn't strike to kill—sufficient life must be left to feed the kiln, though she wonders whether she has already marred his ghost, stained it in pain and terror.

The dome opens, splitting as night does speared by dawn. It is the first time she has seen her audience from this side of the equation. The seats are packed, the faces anonymous, the applause—or whatever it is they are making—a muted roar, unintelligible as the braying of dogs in the hunt. Presiding over them all, distinct, is the queen. Her box a high chamber, her chair no doubt like a throne, and at her side—equally without doubt, though Nuawa can't see through the dark glass— Lussadh, kneeling or standing.

The tournament master's voice, clear and sonorous, declares her the victor. The audience follows, chanting *The Lightning, the Lightning!* Faintly she wonders if her mother is among the spectating mass, aloof, alone of them all to look on with calm certainty while holding the highest stakes.

The box opens and the queen descends, Lussadh not with her after all. The crowd quiets in stages; in the hush, there is a child crying, some colicky baby or unruly toddler too young to comprehend what they see, what this woman-shape represents, what winter is. What any of this signifies. Nuawa imagines assassins in the seats taking aim, measuring the risk. It would be a good opportunity, with a crowd so dense to mask them, so many available exits. But no dart or bullet flies.

The queen does not look at the fallen man, a single body—a single ghost—meriting no attention, though she does step around the blood. She fastens the last victor's badge onto Nuawa's collar, blue-gold hyacinth. "You survived, as I knew you would. And now I suppose you shall join in my service."

Her nerves are singing, electrified independent of her intellect, shivering like a helpless domesticated thing before a predator. Or else it is excitement, intoxicating and buoyant. The body's volatile caprices. She bows her head and gets on her knee, as she has seen Lussadh do. "The highest honor is to serve, Your Majesty."

The crowd takes up their chorus once more. *Absolute winter, absolute winter, absolute winter.*

The royal carriage glides; it feels frictionless from the inside as if moving on air rather than upon a road. Within this confined space, the queen's radiance is inescapable. There is an abundance of wool and furs, but no heating. The only ghosts in the vehicle are for perambulation, set to move and steer the wheels. Nuawa wraps herself in the furs, finding them several sizes too big, and realizes that these are meant for Lussadh. Subtly scented, those oils the general uses, the myrrh. The queen's heart in Lussadh's keeping. She has not contemplated it before. It is an odd thing to dwell upon, though Nuawa finds herself unable to move away from it. Lussadh entwined with that long, pale body, Lussadh's mouth between those long, glacial legs. She wonders whether the general pleasures the queen on her knees every time, or if there is variety in their fucking. Whether their relation is a mirror to hers with Lussadh, or if it is softer. Whether the Winter Queen is capable of tenderness and passion, or even lust.

Nuawa gazes through the sole window, a one-way pane like the arena dome, opaque from the outside. The queen watches her and does not seem interested in conversation until she says, "A long time ago, I had a mirror. This large, the size of my palms put together. No other glass was made like it—indeed, it was fused not from sand but from the ice that resides at a mountain's heart. When you look through it, you can see the world that is now, the world that is beyond, the world that will be. Omniscience, apotheosis. It was a snare for the youthful, the curious, immensely puissant. No forge or fire in the world may melt it."

She doesn't answer; it does not seem she is supposed to, and she means to tread the way she needs on the thinnest of ice.

"It was a treasure, this mirror. It held everything. Not just the sight but the stepping-stone, the pathways. It was as much a door as it was anything else, though you could never guess whether it was one-way or not. That is the problem with thaumaturgy you didn't create yourself." The queen's voice is distant. "But it shattered. I have been looking for its remains since."

Moving fast from the Marrow, the breadth of Sirapirat crossed in no time, made brief and small by this vehicle, the ghosts must be on the finest diet. Sugared candles, expensive incenses, rich broth boiled until it is flavorful steam. Better than some living eat. Nuawa looks out at the gray seam of the thoroughfares, the gunmetal vowels of lampposts, the golden sheen of the mirage. A luminescence that stands in contrast to the queen's. Maybe its dissolution is beyond even her. Some things must be.

"Do you like stories, Nuawa Dasaret?"

"As much as anyone, Your Majesty. The human mind seeks out patterns, applies the structure of beginnings and endings so it may hold onto a sense of order and sequence."

The queen's eyes, black sclera on black irises, are impossible to read. "One of the first children I took in was from the occident. They told a most peculiar tale, that I'd abducted him and tainted him to all that was young and beautiful. A rose-girl journeyed to find him, but she died at sea. A storm—her relatives believed I caused it. It was a pity; I'd have liked to meet her, that brave little creature."

Nuawa puts on another layer of wool. "I've never heard of this story."

"Two, three centuries old, and disseminated in a different part of the world. Continents away, where the sun rises at midnight. Forgotten now; the country was annexed. The tale did have one detail correctly. One to wake. Two to bind. Three—a miracle, a mystery. Is it not strange, do you think, that everything arranges itself into a ritual?"

The queen kisses her. It is chaste, nothing like Lussadh's first, the barest contact of lips on lips. She withdraws and Nuawa abruptly realizes her eyes are not as alien as they initially look; she can discern the outline of irises, the pinpoint pupils like starbursts.

"There," the queen whispers. "Are you afraid? Do you feel tainted?"

The furs are suddenly heavy, too warm. When she shakes them off she finds she is not cold at all, despite the queen's nearness. The detail-work of the carriage stands out in acute relief and the queen likewise, every strand of hair as individual as a brushstroke. The fine bones, clavicles and wrists, like gemstones under a fine silvery cloth. "No," she says, her voice foreign to her, wondering and hushed. Something inside her revolves on an axis she hasn't known existed, as though all this time it has been hibernating and now at last stirs to animation.

"Good." The queen takes her hand.

The rest passes like a dream. She is led up, through parts of the palace that are forbidden to all but the general and the queen, forbidden even to the governor. The passages that have been left untouched, gilded redwood panels and naga statues, mirrors tinted indigo and crimson. She watches her images and the queen's run before and behind them, distorted and cast in red or blue. Her pulse throbs erratically, keeping to a tempo not her own. The queen's tempo.

They come to a heavy door, ebony burnished with bronze, latched in place by a nest of nielloware serpents. Resinous venom collects in a groove, colorless and odorless. Nuawa stops then, slowed by intuition, by premonition that pierces the fog—the royal-kiss haze—which makes her remote and strange to herself. She blinks, alert, her heart hammering. The queen's fingers alight on her shoulder, like her mouth the softest of touches. "Enter. You'll prove yourself. Once is all I require. After that, you'll be one of mine. Among the most powerful of my empire. It is better to be on that end of the equation, isn't it, when the equation is the constant of existence; when you can no more escape it than you can escape the air?"

The vipers disengage, hissing in protest, witched-hunger robbed of yet another meal. Nuawa goes through.

Vahatma. She has seen the god in miniature, icons and amulets. This is twice as tall as she, three times as broad. Even the leopard in their lap is larger than life, nearly double the size of a real animal. Both god and beast are untarnished by time, as lustrous as on the day they were cooling down from the mold.

At the god's feet, her mother. Indrahi leans against Vahatma's bronze knee, eyes shut as though in meditation. Her hands are red, fingers mangled, some of the nails missing. One of her arms is bent impossibly backward. Her lower lip is split.

Nuawa knows she has gone very still. She should show no reaction and yet she cannot move forward. Aloud she says, "Aunt." Is her voice too low, too high, distraught or—as she needs to be—indifferent?

"Ah." The sound is reedy. "There you are. I was always told adopting you as my own would be a terrible mistake, that you'd grow up to be ungrateful and a disappointment. The latter I already realized. The former—tell me, niece, did I raise you so poorly? What have I ever done to you?"

They've cleaned Indrahi so the reek of blood is not high and overwhelming. Underneath that Nuawa smells persimmons, sweet and fresh, the fruit her mother keeps near always but never eats. She used to think it was to do with Tafari, a favorite fruit of her dead parent which Indrahi can no longer bear tasting; she's been forbidden from eating it herself. But she realizes it is for another reason entirely. Her senses, newly honed, catch the acrimonious note. "It's nothing to do with you, Aunt. There is an equation that governs existence and I must fit myself into it, for preference on the side that gains rather than loses. I can be crushed underneath it, or I can lift myself up, away from the soil and the worms of the earth."

From behind her, winter's voice: "Your aunt gave you a piece of my mirror, Nuawa. Even now she will not confess how she came by it or why she concealed it within your heart."

Indrahi lifts her head with difficulty. "Perhaps I met a Yatpun exile, who knew the mountains that birthed you. And perhaps they told me that once you were as small as any snow-woman, least among your kind, ruled beneath the mountain gods' iron thumbs. I know you are doing what you do for a reason. But so am I."

The queen has stepped forward to loom over Indrahi, expressionless, her gown making an iron note against the floor. "You will not provoke me."

"You had sisters." Indrahi is looking at Nuawa as she speaks. "Though your kind don't have parents, the children of permafrost. You emerged from the ice full-grown and you were seized with such curiosity, and the mirror showed you so much you could never have. And now you're finding its pieces to accomplish your heart's desire—"

The queen takes hold of Indrahi's shoulders, lifting her bodily from the ground, an unhuman strength. Then her features ease. She lets go; Indrahi falls with a gasp, a thud. "My error in thinking you would yield something new, here at the last. So be it. Nuawa, the rest is for you."

The poison, Nuawa thinks, must already be halfway through: her mother is dying, would soon wither and rot from within. She doesn't know the composition of what her mother fed the persimmon tree, the additional dosage that might have been added after. The way there was always a persimmon. Thrown out when rotten, replaced with a fresh one, a constant in the drawing room. An insurance against what might one day come. "Your Majesty, my aunt might know more. If you would—" Given time, given opportunity, she can alter this trajectory. No toxin is incurable. No damage to the body is irreparable.

"I have listened enough. Your aunt would bring me harm, making you what you are. She did not tell you. Are you not upset?" The Winter Queen makes a hard gesture. "I will tell you that no curse from fratricide ever takes—not under my protection. Go on."

It is said so simply, even gently. Nuawa stares at the queen, at her mother. Her mother's head stoops as though in exhaustion, in pain, or it may be a nod—purposeful, giving permission. Forgiveness. Nuawa draws her gun, slowly. This may be the best time to test the queen's mortality after all, a fractal bullet will kill most things. Even ghosts, even small gods, and what *is* the queen next to that.

She feels nothing at all, there is only her, alone in her head. The gun is firm in her grip, the metal of it the same as it always has been, agnostic to circumstances and indifferent to emotion. Herself much like it, a human-shaped weapon.

She takes aim. A single shot in the brow, painless, instant. It is a kill, like any other. She imagines she hears the blood pour — a hot brilliant tide, roaring — as she says to the queen, "Will that be all, Your Majesty?"

"Yes." The queen gazes at the body, at the god's shell, and then turns away as though repulsed by this evidence of mortality. Her face seems once more alien, her eyes black, black, black. "That will be all."

TWELVE

THE HOUR, PRE-DAWN, IS SUCH THAT NUAWA EXPECTS NO answer when she knocks on Rakruthai's door. But the doctor is wide awake, if tousled and irritated. "What do you want?" he snaps as he admits Nuawa. "Do you know what time it is?"

"Half past four in the morning." Nuawa wonders how she comes across. She dressed immaculately in the palace; she has not been to her mother's house, for all that it is legally hers now, the greenhouse and the land. On her are the gray and white of winter, the victor's badge at her collar, a belt whose buckle bears the queen's emblem. "I owe you half the pay for the parasite." Albeit it came to no use in the end, unless it might shield her from the sin of matricide.

"Ah." Rakruthai scowls at her clothes. "You won, I hear. Got what you wanted. You'll be quite powerful now, I suppose. Your friends must soon be calling on you."

"They already have." Yifen, Tezem, and even Ziya. A mesh of acquaintances, some barely recalled, sending her notes of congratulations and thinly veiled requests for favors. Nuawa as carrion, and them as an ant swarm. "I'm surprised you aren't."

"I don't care for politics. You're going to be neck-deep in that now." The chiurgeon takes the envelope, opens, counts. There are a few notes extra, but he does not pass remark. "The best thing to do is to keep your head down, survive. But you picked the tightrope. Who knows, maybe it'll suit you. Most likely it will murder you in your sleep. Literally."

"A good point. Is there a way to kill myself slowly, on a schedule?"

His head snaps up from the promissory notes. "What?"

There is a remnant of tobacco in the air, a day or two old, most of it already ventilated through the window. It is not something Nuawa would have noticed before. A gift from the queen, Lussadh might say. "A method that'll kill me in a few years. Let's say eight or ten. I need a motivation, a deadline."

Rakruthai looks at her, perhaps trying to divine by the naked eye whether she has been possessed or gripped by dementia. "I'm a doctor, not an executioner or shaman."

"I can pay you," Nuawa says mildly. "I happen to have inherited some capital overnight." The house will have to be sold or rented out in a year or two. She will make an opportunity to go through it first.

"Fuck off." The doctor shoves the money into a drawer and makes a low, disgusted noise. "I'll give you an anesthesia. It will stunt your parasite's growth so it matures in five years instead of one. By next year it'll be a part of you and removing it will be either painful or fatal. By year five it'll kill you dead, messily, and it'll be pure agony leading up to that. Is that what you want?"

Five years. It is hardly any amount of time. But she will be in the queen's court, part of the queen's defense, close to the throne. If in that time she can do nothing, then nothing can be done. "It sounds very efficient, doctor. I assume in the meantime it'll keep me impervious to curses, grudges, and such?"

"It's in the parasite's interest to keep you healthy. It'll also make you infertile." Rakruthai bends to a bottom drawer, unlocks it, draws out an ivory case. "Take this twice a day. I've measured out the dosages and the dates—dosage has to be higher the further along you go. Miss even one dose and you'll regret it."

"You've always been generous to me. If you ever need anything that's in my power to give ..."

"I'm sending you away with poison." He slams the drawer shut. "I pity your family."

Nuawa's mouth twists. A rictus. "That won't be a problem any longer, since my only meaningful relation is dead. The funeral should be soon, after a fashion. As ever, doctor, I'm grateful." *You're doing what you do now for a reason. But so am I.* Nuawa, six years old, swallowing that sharp, icy fragment. A reason, she thinks. To have her survive, for the queen cannot afford to throw away any piece of her glass? To have her become a possession of winter? A reason.

Outside the day is crisp. After the queen's departure the air is growing, if not warm, then less frigid. The general is waiting for her by the carriage. "Lieutenant," Lussadh says. The general cuts a sharp figure in gray and white, coat fresh and spotless, belt a gleaming black slash. Her hair is tied at the nape of her neck, caught in a platinum band that, like much else, bears the queen's hyacinth.

She salutes—this requires no learning; she's seen the gesture many times over since childhood, a hand over her heart to signify devotion to the queen. "You didn't have to pick me up. I'm just a soldier."

"I have got your luggage. We'll be leaving this afternoon. You have settled all your affairs?"

"Some loose legalistic ends, but I don't anticipate them being an issue. It's not as though I will never come back to Sirapirat." Five years, Nuawa thinks. She will mark each day—each hour— with precision, balancing it in an account.

On Lussadh's urging she looks over her belongings, a couple suitcases, the sum and total of her material life. Atop them, folded neatly, is her mother's diptych. She pulls it over, props it up in her lap. It is cumbersome. She parts it enough to feel the paint, the canvas. Breathes in the smell. Her throat closes and she thinks that she must burn it, to prove a point.

"I realize you didn't get along well with your aunt," the general is saying, "but she said she wanted you to have it, not that you are obliged to."

"I'll take it with me." Nuawa draws in a breath, feigns a cough, clears her throat. Her limbs ache, as though grief translates itself to physical hurt. Nausea at the back of her mouth. "An antique. I've never understood why she kept it around, but it might prove valuable one day."

Lussadh does not ask how she feels or offer her condolences. She wonders whether the general understands her better than most, or if there is a distinction because the general ended the al-Kattan line on her own volition. But the general does put an arm around her. Nuawa says, "Am I going to share your quarters, over there?"

"If you wish, it would be my delight." The general kisses her palm. "You're remarkable."

In what, Nuawa wonders. In reptilian ruthlessness. In the ability to carry out matricide and act like nothing of import has happened, after. Their one common ground then, this deficit in humanity. Someday she will have to find out if the mirror shards are attracted to monsters in the making or if the glass makes them that way, sanding off empathy and compassion. "I'm glad you think so, General." She presses her brow to the window, smudging it. A new day. Not even winter can stop the passage of sunrise, the warmth, the brilliance it brings. In another part of the world, spring or summer is beginning.

Nothing is forever. Even winter can end; even the queen can fall.

Nuawa puts the diptych away. To Lussadh she says, "I look forward to serving the queen with you, General."

A slow nod. Another kiss, this time on her lips. "To her eternal reign."

"To your grace," Nuawa says against the general's mouth, "and to absolute winter."

ABOUT THE AUTHOR

Benjanun Sriduangkaew writes love letters to strange cities, beautiful bugs, and the future. Her work has appeared on Tor.-com, *Beneath Ceaseless Skies*, *Clarkesworld*, *Apex Magazine*, and year's best collections. She has been shortlisted for the Campbell Award for Best New Writer, and her debut novella Scale-Bright has been nominated for the British SF Association Award.

For more information:
https://beekian.wordpress.com/

THE
KRAKEN SEA

A fast paced adventure full of mystery, Fates, and writhing tentacles just below the surface, and in the middle of it all is a boy searching for himself

"Tobler creates a fluid, transformative universe that's equal parts exhilaration and terror."
Publishers Weekly (Starred Review)

"Richly experimental horror."
Locus Magazine

E. CATHERINE TOBLER

CPSIA information can be obtained
at www.ICGtesting.com
Printed in the USA
FSHW010506140121
77687FS